ZODIAC LOVERS

Paranormal Romance

Book Three

LEO ✳ VIRGO ✳ LIBRA

LANCE TAUBOLD

Print and Digital Editions
Copyright 2018
Discover new and exciting works published by Invoke Books at
InvokeBooks.com

DEDICATION

FOR MY TOOTSIE AND DAD:

63 YEARS TOGETHER AND BEYOND.

A TRUE PARANORMAL ROMANCE.

TABLE OF CONTENTS

LEO

The Lion

Traits: Generous, Warm-Hearted, Enthusiastic, Creative, Broad-minded, Faithful, Loving, Dogmatic, Intolerant

Ireland

10 years ago

"Come on, Bry. It's not Mt. Everest. It's only a hill, for God's sake. I can see the cathedral from here," Key Durham shouted to his best friend, who was a good football-field's length behind him. He could see the mist around the ruins of the cathedral just ahead.

"The Rock of Cashel. Or as it was also known, Cashel of the Kings. Cashel means stronghold," Key espoused to his best friend of ten years, Bryan Benton, as he caught up, huffing a bit.

Bryan was 6' 2" and 220 lbs. of hard muscle—and obnoxiously proud of it. Narcissistic was the word for Bryan. And if it wasn't for his crazy, good-naturedness, and his bronzed, Irish good looks, he would be intolerable. He did have a caring side and Key loved him for it, and if it wasn't for Bryan, he would never have agreed to go to Ireland to celebrate their college graduation.

"It'll be awesome, Key. All those hot Irish guys. All that Guiness. It'll be two weeks of drunken debauchery!" Bryan had told him two months before graduation. "I'll make sure you get laid. I mean, there oughta be *someone* who'll sleep with you." Bryan had laughed. "If not, I can always throw you one of my pity fucks. You're not too bad in the sack... and if I get drunk enough." He'd laughed again, referring to their two-month affair in their junior year. They hadn't been in love—they both knew it—but they'd also both

2

recognized their lust for one another. It had been fun. And now they could look back and joke about it.

"Maybe we can find you a hot leprechaun. Although, that's kind of an oxymoron since leprechauns are gross. I bet they have little twisty leprechaun dicks, all gnarly and shit." Bryan twisted his fingers in front of Key's face as he said it. "But hey, gnarly dick's better than no dick."

"Okay, asshole, what makes you think I can't get laid?" Key punched Bryan in the chest. "I know you think you're God's gift to the world of men—gay *and* straight—but I do all right."

"You're righ—"

"Thank you."

"I am God's gift to the world of men—gay *and* straight. My big chest, my big arms—"

"Your big ego. That and your dick—which isn't *that* big—are going to get you in *big* trouble someday. Now, can we drop this? We didn't come three thousand miles and trek up this hill to discuss your inflated ego and sexual prowess. I wanna explore. Besides which, people will be here soon. That's why I wanted to get here right before dawn: no people, and we can explore on our own first."

"Fine." Bryan was duly chastened, then added, "We can talk about me later." He playfully tapped Key on the shoulder."

"Incorrigible," Key muttered. "Up there at the end is where I want to go." He pointed to the far right end of the ruined building. "That's the sanctuary part with the cross, where it's all misty still."

"It looks creepy."

Key could hear the genuine consternation in Bryan's voice and decided to use it. "Oh, Big Bad Bryan is all afraid of a little fog," he said querulously. "Wait! Can you hear that?" He grabbed Bryan's biceps and felt him stiffen. "I hear a wailing. Like a... a... banshee!" He squeezed Bryan's arm harder. Bryan was frozen, eyes wide. "Oh. It's just the wind." He released his grip and strode off to the church.

"You're a *prick*, you know that, Durham? I'll get you for that. Forget getting laid. I'm gonna cock-block you every chance I get. Your blue-balls will be *black*. I'm gonna fuck my brains out and all you're gonna do is watch... and that's if I let you even do *that*. And what's a banshee?"

Bryan was ranting to air, as Key had gone into the ruin and couldn't be seen.

"Hey, Bryan, you gotta see this. It's so cool!" Key yelled from somewhere in the crumbling edifice.

Bryan grumblingly trudged into the ancient church. "Where are you, Key? I can't see a fucking thing in this soup. Has it gotten hotter? I'm glad we wore only T-shirts. I'm sweating."

"Over here." Key's voice came from off to Bryan's right. "The mist is thinner here."

Bryan slowly made his way, eyes squinting, hands brushing away mist as if it was curtains. A hand came out of the mist and grabbed his forearm. "*AHH!*"

"It's only me, Bryan. Jeez, you screamed like a girl. Wait'll I tell all your would-be guy-fucks that you're just a big, screaming, girly fag. We'll see who gets cock-blocked now."

"You wouldn't dare." Bryan yanked his arm away.

"Try me, fag boy. Come on, I gotta show you something." Key grabbed Bryan's hand and led him off.

The mist began to clear and they could see the outline of a stone cross.

"That's St. Patrick's Cross. It was built to commemorate St. Patrick's visit to baptize the king around 450 A. D. There's this cool legend about the Devil getting angry at Patrick and putting a curse on the people here."

"Curse?" Trepidation crept into Bryan's voice again.

"Yeah, something about the Devil was all pissed off one time and in a fit of anger over St. Patrick building a new church here, so he took a bite out of the Slieve Bloom Mountains, which surround this area, and spit it out right here, creating the Rock also called The Devil's Bit."

"Bullshit."

"You're so eloquent, Bryan. Anyway, they built the church and crowned all the old kings of Ireland here. There are some time discrepancy stories about it all, but this was the place until 978 A. D.— you'll like this part—and Brian Boru, the greatest king of Ireland, was crowned here, and he made this, Cashel, his home. Boru joined all the tribes of Ireland together for the first time and ruled from this spot until 1014. Then his descendants ruled for another hundred years or so, until the Catholic Church took over the place and made it a cathedral. Now here's the really sad part. In 1647, some Earl Inchquin guy, under Cromwell, attacked the city, but all the townsfolk had barricaded themselves in the Cathedral. Inchquin burned the Cathedral and killed all eight hundred people. After that, it was abandoned."

Bryan was silent, rapt.

"They say the whispering sounds here are the poor peoples' ghosts, wailing as they burned–their souls trapped here forever." Key paused. "I wonder if that's the sound I heard before?"

Bryan stared, mesmerized. He looked at Key, then said, "You-are-an-*ASSHOLE*!" He shoved Key hard.

Key fell back and hit his head on the stone cross's pedestal and fell to the ground.

Bryan's eyes widened. "*Key!* Are you all right?"

Then he noticed the blood on the pedestal.

Key didn't respond. He lay with eyes closed.

Bryan bent to Key and raised his head slowly. He felt the wet slickness on the back of Key's head.

A groan.

"Key, I'm so sorry," Bryan said. "I didn't mean to hurt you. Are you okay? Can you talk?"

Key put out his hand and tried to raise himself up. "Yeah, I think so. I'll probably have a knot back there though."

"I've got an extra T-shirt in my backpack. We can wipe up the blood with it. There doesn't seem to be too much." Bryan slipped off the small backpack he'd been carrying. "See, and you told me not to lug it with me." He unzipped the pack and withdrew the shirt. He gently eased it onto the back of Key's head. "You'll be okay."

"Yeah, I feel a little better, already." Key sat up and held the shirt to his head. "Of course, if you hadn't pushed me I wouldn't need your ratty old T-shirt."

"Hey, I said I'm sorry. And I've only worn the shirt a couple of times. You can keep it." Bryan laughed a little.

"You're such a jerk sometimes... most of the time." Key tried to stand. "Are you gonna help me up? I think the bleeding's stopped. There's not that much. I only grazed the rock." He inspected the shirt.

"Sure. Let me see." Bryan took the shirt and inspected Key's head. "Yep. It's stopped. And you're still your gorgeous self." He kissed Key on the forehead. "Forgive me?"

"Yeah. Just don't do it again."

"Promise. I guess sometimes my massive muscles are too much." Bryan flexed his biceps and held the pose.

"No. *You* are too much," Key said, glaring at Bryan.

"Your head okay?" genuine concern in Bryan's voice. "I think you got blood on the altar. Like a blood sacrifice." He inspected the pedestal.

"Shit. Maybe we should wipe it off. Here use your T-shirt."

As Bryan wiped/smeared the blood off the pedestal, Key noticed a break in the mist to the right ahead of them.

"Hey, Bryan, look over there. There's a clear spot in the mist, like a tunnel."

"Cool. But creepy, too." Bryan stuffed the T-shirt back into his pack and made no move to follow Key.

Key rolled his eyes. "Mister Tough-Guy. Let's go."

"Maybe we should go back so you can lie down. You might have a concussion or something."

Key was surprised at Bryan's reticence. "I'm fine. Why don't you want to go on?"

"I don't know." Bryan's voice quieted. "It doesn't feel right. Something's weird and wrong. I mean, a tunnel of clear space in the fog? What is that? Let's look around the rest of the place instead, if you don't want to go back."

"You're crazy, Bry. Okay, I agree, it's kind of weird, but we came all this way to explore, and I really want to see what's there. It might be something really cool. It looks like it goes off down the hill. It's something special, Bry. Like us, right? Come on, please. For me? It's the least you can do after almost killing me on that rock. Here. I'll hold your hand." Key grabbed Bryan's hand and began to lead him.

Bryan stumbled a couple of steps forward. "Fine. But anything weird happens, Durham, and we're outta there." He shuffled along, firmly holding Key's hand. "And no more of that banshee shit. Promise?"

"I promise." Key turned away from Bryan to hide his smile. *Tough guy.*

They walked along the crease of light in the mist for several hundred feet until the path began to angle down the side of the hill.

"Hey, I think I see a town or something up ahead. I don't remember the book saying anything about a town. I thought it was all just the Tipperary Plain. They call it the Golden Vale, you know, but

I guess that must be when there's no fog." Key tugged Bryan's hand. "Come on, Bry, stop dragging your feet. The mist is clearing."

"About fucking time. Stop pulling so hard. We're not in a hurry or anything." Bryan picked up his pace a little. "You're right. It does look like a town. An *old* town."

"It's Ireland. There's tons of old shit here. And look, it's clearing up. Do you want me to stop holding your hand Big Boy?" Key smiled at Bryan.

"You know you only held my hand 'cuz *you* wanted to. It was just your excuse to say that you thought *I* was afraid so you could touch me." Bryan yanked Key to him; their chests bumped." He put his forehead to Key's.

"Will you knock it off? I've got a headache—thanks to you." Key pulled away.

"Sorry. Hey, I'm thirsty. I could use a beer. I hope this place has got a pub." Then he added to Key's departing back, "Maybe I'll let you do me later."

"Not gonna happen, Bry. That ship has sailed," Key said over his shoulder. "I'm over your self-proclaimed sexy body and good looks. Time to move on, bigger and better, maybe someone a little more substantial. Muscles and a big dick aren't everything, you know." He continued walking.

"Yes they are. That's why you love me." Bryan increased his pace to catch up. "Come on, Key, wait up. And there's nobody bigger or better."

"Give it up, Bry," As they progressed, Key noted a couple of small wood-and-stone buildings along the path, for it certainly couldn't be called a road. It was all dirt. Hadn't they heard of asphalt? Still, it was kind of quaint. Key saw some smoke coming from one of the larger buildings up ahead. A door opened and two men stepped out, apparently deep in conversation. Key called out, "Good morning."

The men stopped and stared at them, mouths dropping open. They looked at one another and scurried away down the path.

"That was kind of rude," Key said. "I thought the Irish were all so friendly."

"Yeah, well, not everybody is charmed by your boyish good looks and wavy black hair. And did you see their weird clothes? It's like they were peasants or something. I don't think this is a happening place, but I do think that might be the local pub they just came out of. I'm parched. And hungry. I hope they've got food. I could go for one of those Irish breakfasts. Speaking of which, I don't know how these people can eat all that food every day and not weigh, like, four hundred pounds. I eat a lot, but shit, they're crazy." Bryan approached the door to the pub.

"They eat like that because they're all farmers and laborers. They need to keep up their strength—*real strength*—not show muscles." Key punched Bryan's chest for emphasis. "Open the door."

"Yeah, but I put on a good show." Bryan rubbed his chest. "And stop punching me. What's all this aggression?"

"Must be the clean Irish air. Open the door, Bry. I can't get around you.

Bryan grabbed the door handle and stepped back. "After you, my Lord."

"Fuck off. And try to behave. I don't want to get thrown out of, probably, the only pub in town." Key walked through the door.

"I'll be on my best behavior."

"That's what I'm afraid of," Key said. "Be cool. I know you can do it if you try. Let's just have fun."

"Let's have fun then, my best buddy." He patted Key on the back and followed him through the old wooden door into the pub.

The bar was medium-sized and typical old world. An all-wood bar, ten or so wood stools, non-matching, were bellied-up. Four patrons were bellied-up as well. Eight small wood tables were haphazardly strewn around the room. Four or five men were also haphazardly strewn at the tables. A dulled mirror lined the back of the thirty-foot or so length of the bar, several wooden kegs at one end. Quite a few, seemingly unlabeled, bottles lined the back of the bar.

All the patrons and bartender were dressed similarly in dark-colored peasantish clothing, with the exception of two very tall men at the far end of the bar. They seemed better dressed and groomed than the others.

"Check out the two guys at the far end. They look pretty good from here," Bryan said from Key's side as they took a few steps toward a table near the door.

"Bryan, don't you even notice that everyone *but* those two

guys is staring at us?"

"Well, of course. We're fresh blood. This doesn't exactly seem like a tourist hot spot." Bryan tapped Key's arm. "Hey, *now* they're looking."

Key glanced across the bar at the two men, openly staring. They were incredibly handsome. Long, wavy, black hair, burnished skin, patrician features—refined, yet swarthy—an odd, devastating combination. Key couldn't take his eyes off them. They were—

"Twins. Key, they're *twins*." Bryan tapped Key's arm more vigorously now. "Super-hot twins."

"Shh, Bryan. They'll hear you."

"I think that warning's too late. Here they come."

The two men strode—swaggered, Key thought—over to them. Both were tall, at least six-three or four. All in black. Their shirts and pants were different in style from the rest of the locals— almost modern. *Very odd.* Their gazes were penetrating, hypnotic. Dangerous. As they approached the table, Key could see that their eyes were as black as their hair. Midnight in a coal mine. They were broad-shouldered, broad-chested, with tapering waists. Models of masculine perfection.

The twins stopped at their table.

Hands proffered, "Welcome. I'm Luc," the one on Key's right said. "I'm Dev," said the other. Both Bryan and Key exchanged handshakes with them.

"Great to meet you," Bryan said, still shaking the hand of the one on the left—Dev's. "You're twins."

"Way to go, Bry. Master of the obvious," Key said. "Forgive my friend. He only recently graduated college." He tried to make light of Bryan's gaffe.

"It's charming," Dev said, maintaining Bryan's grip and giving the hint of a smile.

"Can we buy you gentlemen a drink?" the other one, Luc, asked, getting Key's attention.

"Um, sure." Key said.

Without losing eye contact with Key, Luc raised an arm and snapped his fingers, apparently at the barkeep, as an older man behind the bar scurried to a tap.

"You guys must be from around here. We're from Boston. Massachusetts, that is, I'm Bryan, like Boru, right Key?" Bryan said.

"Remember what I said about embarrassing me?" Key elbowed Bryan in the side. "Sit."

Bryan and Key sat, the twins did also. "I'm Key, and Bryan and I were up the hill at the Rock of Cashel. It was pretty foggy, but we saw this path down the hill and it led us here. Which is where, by the way?"

The old barkeep suddenly appeared with four metal steins and set them on the table. "Milord," the slightly stooped man said and bowed his greyed head slightly.

The twins didn't acknowledge the man, but Key said, "Thank you."

The barkeep barely paused, slicing his eyes to Key with an odd look, then quickly hustled away.

"To new friends," Dev said, raising his stein and giving Bryan an intense stare.

"Friends," Luc gave the same stare to Key.

"Friends works for me," Bryan said toasting. "For now."

Key saw the three look at him, waiting for him to say something. The word "friends" coming from the mouths of the twins seemed to connote anything but friendship. It was unsettling. "Slainte," Key said, using the Gaelic toasting word for Good Health.

"Aye, a true Irishman," Luc said, now with a heavy Irish lilt.

"Wow. That was good," Bryan said. "Very cool... and sexy. You should talk like that all the time."

"*Bryan...*" Key admonished.

"Well, it is cool," Bryan said defensively.

"I'm glad ye enjoy it, me lad," Dev now said, full accent flourishing. He winked very suggestively at Bryan and took a long pull of his beer.

Bryan gulped audibly, gazing at Dev, joining him in a draught.

"How long are ye lads staying?" Dev asked Bryan after swallowing."

"Or how long would ye like to stay?" Luc said to Key, without a not-so-subtle subtext. He raised his arm again and snapped for more beers.

Key was disconcerted. Things were getting too intense. "I don't think I could have another beer. I can already feel this one. I think they're stronger here, or maybe we just need to eat. I'm starving. Bryan?" He nudged his friend. "*You* said *you* were starving before we got here."

Bryan pulled out of his trance with Dev. "What? Oh yeah. Starving. I could eat something." He looked back at Dev.

The implication seemed to not be lost on Dev, who openly smiled at Bryan and said, "Then let us slake your hunger, me fine lad." Dev raised his hand and snapped his fingers.

The barkeep was approaching the table with their second round.

"Breakfast," Dev said, not looking at the man.

The man nodded and hurried away.

Key was feeling railroaded by the twins and needed to get some kind of control. He knew Bryan was already smitten, but perhaps he could de-escalate the situation some. "This beer has gone right through me. Where's the restroom?" he asked Luc.

"Aye. The restroom. That would be out through the door at the back. I'll show you," Luc said, getting up.

"No, that's all right," Key hurried to say. "I'm sure I can find it. Bryan, I'm *sure* you need it, too." He tugged Bryan's elbow.

"I'm good," Bryan said, trying to shrug off Key's death-grip.

"No, you're not. Come on." Key pulled him up.

Bryan gave an unintelligible huff. "Fine. Don't go anywhere," he said to Dev, leaning over to him, their foreheads almost touching.

"I won't," Dev almost whispered, leaving his lips parted in temptation, then rolled his tongue over his bottom lip.

Key watched this exchange with disgust and yanked Bryan's arm hard before things got crazy. He waited until they'd exited through a small door at the back of the bar, assuming this was the right way, as it was the only other door in the place.

They found themselves outside again.

"Hey, I don't want to leave," Bryan said, releasing himself from Key's grasp.

"I think that little shack there is the toilet," Key said, pointing to a broken-down four-by-four, planked structure off to the right.

"You're kidding, right?" Bryan said. "My shoulders won't fit through the doorway. I'll have to piss sideways."

"You don't have to piss, anyway. I just wanted to talk to you," Key said. "What was that thing that Dev guy did with his tongue? Really, Bryan. There's something wrong with those twins."

"Are you nuts? That tongue thing was *hot*. They're perfect."

"Yeah, a little too perfect. Did you notice how nobody looked at them or talked to them... like they were afraid or something? And in the middle of nowhere, a little village no less, we happen to find two great-looking guys who are also gay? I mean, this is the new millennium and all, but this place looks like hundreds of years ago. I don't think they've caught up with the times."

"So it's a coincidence. Big deal. They happen all the time. Listen, Key, if you don't wanna join in the fun, okay. But don't wreck it for me. It's my dream come true. I always wanted to make it with twins. *Hot* twins."

"Fine, Bryan. Have fun, but don't say I didn't warn you. Be careful what you wish for and all that. It just might bite you in the ass."

"That's what I'm hoping for... and a lot of other places, too. Now, come on. Let's have another beer, buddy. Maybe you'll change your mind." Bryan put his arm around Key's shoulder and led him back into the bar.

"Lads, we were coming to look for ya. Thought you might have got lost," Dev said, pushing out a stool so Bryan could sit. "I ordered another round for ya."

"Thanks, Dev," Bryan said, sitting. "More lubrication's always good." He laughed at his own joke.

Key was about to say something when the door opened and in walked a man. Not just a man, Key observed, but an incredibly masculine force. Tall, long, reddish-blond hair, ruddy complexion, powerfully built. Key was stricken. *Another one? What did they eat here? Three great looking guys in one place? Weirder and weirder?* But this man was different from the twins. He had a commanding presence, but there also seemed to be a softness, a compassion in him. He couldn't explain it; he sensed it. The man's eyes quickly swept the room, alighting on Key.

Their eyes met. Key was spellbound. The man strode to Key, never losing his gaze.

Key saw the mesmerizing eyes, green with flecks of gold. Devastating. Key judged him to be about thirty or so.

"I heard we had newcomers," the throaty baritone voice said.

Everyone else at the table was quiet. Key found his voice and prayed it wouldn't crack. "I'm Key."

"Teague. Teague McLaren." He proffered his hand to Key.

Key took it and felt a grip of fire and strength—not painful—assertive. "This is my friend Bryan."

Teague smiled and shook Bryan's hand as well. "Pleased to meet you, laddie. Welcome to Cashel."

"Same here," Bryan said, cranking a little too much on Teague's hand. "And this is..."

"I know them." Teague said coldly, not looking at or acknowledging the twins.

Key stared at the twins. They were staring at Teague with a look bordering on malevolence. *No love lost there,* Key noted.

"How long are ye here for? Perhaps ye'd like to see the town? The town's wee, but the countryside's lovely."

Key would go anywhere with this man, and what a perfect excuse to leave the twins, breakfast or no. "We'd love to, Teague. Thanks for the beers, guys. Let's go, Bryan."

"Whoa, what's the rush?" Bryan said. "We can't just rush off. I haven't finished my beer, and we have breakfast coming." He glared meaningfully at Key.

Key knew there was no way Bryan would leave. His dick had spoken. "Fine. I'm not really hungry, and I've had enough beer. It's gotten to me already."

"Aye, me grandda pours a mean draught," Teague said and waved at the barkeep for emphasis.

The old man raised a hand in return, seemed to lock eyes for a moment too long with Teague, gave a slight nod, and went back to polishing the bar.

"That's your grandfather?" Key said.

"Aye," Teague said. "He's been here for..." Teague paused, trying to find words, "many years."

Key noticed the twins had been strangely quiet throughout the whole interchange, as if they weren't there—which was fine with Key. "Well, let's go then," he said. "I'll see you later, Bry. I guess we'll meet back here." He put a hand on Bryan's shoulder and looked him dead in the eye. "Be careful."

"Always." Bryan smirked. "Don't wait up for me."

"Cute. Remember what I said. I'm ready, Teague."

Teague put a friendly arm around Key's shoulder and led him away from the threesome.

Key suddenly felt the urge not to leave Bryan, that it would be mistake. He glanced back at the twins, who were now on either side of Bryan. Each had a hand on Bryan's thighs, shoulders joined together in intimacy. Hyenas ready to pounce on their weak prey. Key hesitated in his progression to the door. "Maybe I should stay."

Solemnly, Teague said, "It would do no good, lad. He's made his choice."

Key still hesitated, taking in the almost obscene tableau of Bryan and the twins. Teague was right. There was no changing Bryan's mind. He'd been baited, hooked, and caught. Key said a silent prayer. *Please let him be all right.* He gave Teague a spurious smile. "Let's go see Cashel."

Key and Teague walked through the town—such as it was— maybe half a dozen wooden and thatched buildings. All were quite small and seemed to have little purpose. Key asked, "Have you lived here long?" Then realized that he must sound as inane as Bryan.

Teague seemed not to notice the inanity and responded, "All my twenty-eight years."

"I'm twenty-one." Then Key felt he had to add, "I'm gay."

"I can tell." Teague smiled. "I try to be as happy as I can be, also."

Key laughed a little. "No. Gay. Like, I like other guys... gay."

"Ah." Teague nodded his head. "Well, in that case, me lad, I'm 'gay,' also."

Key stopped walking and turned to Teague. "Wait a minute. Is everyone here gay? Not that it's a bad thing. On the contrary. I mean, I'm really glad you're gay. It's just, you, those twin guys... I mean, what are the chances." Key realized he was rambling and hoped that Teague understood.

"Ye're a charmin' lad, ye are. And to answer your questions, if that's what they were, no, everyone's not gay. Although, I do like the word. There are a few fellas here that are. Is it unusual where you come from?"

"America? It's a big place. But in proportion, there's about one in four, they say. It just seems strange I've run into three already in the first hour. *And* they're all stupid-hot." Key felt himself blush, as he realized what he'd said.

"Aye, charmin' fer sure. But I dinna ken what you meant by 'stupid-hot'?"

Key was mortified. Now he had to *explain* that he thought

Teague was knockout gorgeous? Teague stared at him waiting for an answer. Intense emerald eyes bore into him. He cleared his throat and tried to be matter-of-fact. "Well, it means, like, you know, really good-looking—hot—sizzling, smoking, crazy, ridiculously sexy, hunky... Please help me here. I wanna crawl in a hole. I've never felt so awkward. Must've been the beer or the air or something."

Teague was chuckling softly. "I think I understand now."

Key watched Teague's eyes darken and his face become serious.

Then it happened.

Teague leaned over and pressed his lips to Key's.

Time stopped. The air evaporated around them. Key was transfixed. Soft lips merged with his own, melting his entire body into one gelatinous sensation of pleasure. He put his arms around Teague and felt hot, hard muscle. Teague's back muscles rippled in such a sensual way that Key wanted to explore it with his fingers forever.

Then it stopped.

Teague pulled back and slowly pushed Key's arms down and away from him. Key held them at his side. Frozen. Teague slowly smiled with sensuality, then whispered. "I was going to apologize for kissin' ye out where everyone can see... but I wouldna be sincere. I'm not sorry a'tall. Ye're a bewitchin' lad." He leaned in for one more quick kiss. "Aye. Stupid-hot."

"Wow. I need to sit down. This is crazy. Can we go somewhere?" Key looked around at... a lot of nothing. "And not to the pub. I don't want to see those guys again."

Teague's face hardened. "Ye won't. I'll make sure of it. To the left up ahead. There's a path that leads to a field of heather and buttercups and clover. It's beautiful. We can sit there."

Key heaved a sigh. "Sounds great. Let's just get away from here."

They walked for several yards, rounded a bend, and Key felt his hand being taken by Teague.

It felt right. *Stupid-right.* Key stifled the impulse to pull Teague to him and kiss him again.

They walked in silence for a few minutes, enjoying each other's presence. Key would glance at Teague and smile, and Teague would in turn smile back and gaze intently at Key.

"Over this ridge," Teague said. "It's my favorite place."

They crested the ridge and Key looked out on an expanse of intense color.

It was a purple and yellow and white blanket of soft beauty. A never ending sea of blooms in a vale of fantasy.

Key drew in a quick breath. "I've never seen anything so beautiful before. It's magical."

"Aye. I believe so. I'm glad ye like it. Where would ye like to sit?" Teague asked a rapt Key.

"Here. Right here. We can see it all. I love this." Key sat and pulled Teague down with him, crushing clover and heather. He looked straight forward and said out to the field, "What's happening? What are you doing to me?"

Teague looked at him. "Ye stole my very thoughts. There is more going on here than either of us can explain. But I have to tell ye, I've never felt like this before. I didn't think it was possible. Not after everything that's—" Teague left the final thought in the air.

"Everything that's what? Tell me. I know something's happening here. I know I was meant to be here... with you, but I don't understand it. I'm scared. I want you. You make me feel things I've read and dreamed about, but I'm so confused." He buried his face in Teague's chest, glorying in the masculine scent.

Teague held Key to him, caressing his shoulders and back. "Laddie, ye could not be more confused than I. I burn for ye." He pulled Key's head up, looked fervently into his eyes, and lowered his head to Key's.

This was what Key had been waiting for... perhaps his whole life. This was the fulfillment he needed. This was the man he needed. This was... love?

As their lips and tongues melded, a thought burgeoned in Key's addled brain. *How could it be?* What was he doing? This gorgeous hunk of an Irishman had bowled him over. Had taken control and made him feel things he'd never felt before. And this was just from kissing! He needed to stop this right now. He pulled away and said, "I can't do this. You're great and everything, but we just met. I don't do this. I'm not Bryan. I... I..." The look in Teague's eyes undid him. The vulnerability, the hurt, the... love? was more than he could take. "You don't know me. I don't know you. This is just..."

Teague pulled him close, firmly planting his lips on Key's.

They remained that way for a few seconds, until Teague said, "Right. This is just right, laddie. Ye know it. I know it. Sometimes there is a force more powerful than we can ken. Trust it."

The fervent look in Teague's eyes conveyed it all. Key paused for a moment, staring into this beautiful man's face, looking for a glitch, or doubt, or one speck of hesitation. There was none. This was real. He trusted Teague. Now, he needed to trust himself. Teague lay on his back staring up at him. Waiting. The look on his face, raw. Key made his decision.

This is *right. For whatever reason, this is right.* Key slowly lowered his head to Teague's.

"Aye, laddie."

Their lips met. But this time there was no hesitation. Key opened his mouth and fully accepted Teague's anxious tongue. His hands slid under Teague's coarse linen shirt and met the hard flesh underneath.

Key kneaded Teague's firm chest, brushed the hardened nipples, then pinched them to awareness.

Teague wriggled beneath him, thrusting his chest into Key's palms, moaning with the pleasure he received.

Key was caught up in his power, lost in the control he had over this pliant, virile man. This man was relinquishing his control to him. Key was shaken, yet excited. He needed to feel the rest of him. He thrust his hands downward, and in a quick movement, shoved the rough shirt over Teague's broad shoulders, and placed it behind his head, affording a little ground covering. Teague, similarly, ran his hands beneath the bottom of Key's T-shirt and furiously removed it over Key's head, letting it land where it might in the verdant vale. Key flinched.

"What's wrong, laddie?"

"Nothing," Key said. "I hit my head on the pedestal this morning." He reached behind his head, felt a slight lump. "See, no blood. It only bled a little, really. It was Bryan's fault; he shoved me and I fell. I'm fine now."

Key saw Teague's body momentarily stiffen and an odd look came into his eyes.

"Don't be mad. We were just fooling around. I'm fine. Really." Key hesitated before saying, "I need you."

Teague's eyes burned anew and he pulled Key to him.

Their flesh met, a scorching, burning sensation. Key gasped; Teague gasped. Their mouths joined in a flurry of lips and tongues.

Key's hands roamed maniacally over Teague's taut torso.

Teague seemed to be caught up in the same wave of desire.

Hundreds of hands were everywhere.

Key needed more. His hips were moving frantically over Teague's as if the incessant writhing could give them their desired release.

Their intoxicating sweat and the plentiful scents from the wildflowers made an impossibly seductive permutation.

Suddenly, Teague stopped and abruptly stood, his breathing a series of harsh gasps. He looked at Key with an intensity as if he were forging steel.

Key knew the intention. He unbuckled his belt, undid his jeans and rapidly slid them and his briefs down his body, baring his desire.

Teague's eyes darkened to a deep emerald intensity, taking in the man lying before him. Key put his jeans behind him on the ground. Teague picked up the underwear, cocked his at them and held them to his face. "Very nice." He handed them to Key, who put them behind his head as he lay back to stare up—waiting. Teague undid the cord at his waist and divested himself of his pants. He stood upright, holding the coarse pants in front of his center, then cavalierly let them drop, letting Key's gaze linger over his nakedness.

Key had never seen a man so jaw-droppingly perfect. He took in the fine dusting of blond hair that covered his chest, trailing perfectly in a V down his torso—an arrow pointing to the pot of gold. The same colored wisps of hair covered his powerful legs, neither of which detracted from Key's main focus of the large endowment thrusting haughtily from a darkened blond thatch of hair just below Teague's waist.

Teague, hands on hips, spoke huskily, taking in Key's obvious desire, "I see we have much in common, laddie."

Key would normally have felt uncomfortable, lying naked in front of someone, but with Teague it felt natural. He gave a wry look to Teague and said, "Aye." He extended an arm to Teague, grasped his hand and pulled him down.

Teague's body covered Key's. Key gloried in the full weight of the man pressed onto him. Teague slowly gyrated his lower body over Key's. Their erections rubbed together, hips ground into one another, coarse hairs sensitized everywhere, hot mouths interlocked, tongues melded. Pure erotic sensation.

Teague's lips moved to Key's ear, licking a slow trail along his jaw line. A raspy whisper, "Laddie, I want to pleasure ye."

Key felt the hot breath in his ear, as teeth nibbled and tongue-licked his lobe. "Yes," he gasped, twisting his neck, allowing Teague's mouth better access.

Teague's tongue began its descent, back down his jaw line to Key's shoulder—more licking and nibbling. Key felt his hand being put behind his head. Teague's worked his tongue over the top of Key's shoulder, along his biceps, stopping at the crook of his bent arm, then trailing underneath onto his triceps and into his armpit. Key knew he wasn't exactly Irish Spring fresh after his hard trek up the hill, but that didn't seem to matter to Teague—to the contrary, it seemed to inspire him.

"I like your smell, laddie."

Key moaned again as Teague's tongue continued its exploration.

"And taste."

Key grasped Teague's head fast to him in under his arm, lost in the exquisite feeling.

Teague fervently set to work, making Key groan even more. Then Teague paused, raised his head, and stared passionately into Key's eyes. Key stared at the wet, full lips above him as they slowly lowered to join his own, tongues meshing and molding. The salty, sweaty taste of himself combined with Teague's own erotic flavor were almost more than he could bear, and he knew he couldn't last long if this continued.

As if sensing Key's torment, Teague doubled his efforts, tongue and hands ravishing Key's upper body all the while Teague increased the movement of his lower body over Key's. Once again Teague returned to Key's mouth, and he whispered, "Go ahead, laddie," came the Irish whisper, as fingers closed over Key's nipples and Teague's mouth devoured his.

Key felt the penultimate build, as he thrust his hips upward. Then he screamed into Teague's mouth and the eruption rocked him, wave after endless wave of pleasure.

After a couple of minutes, Key's body calmed somewhat as he basked in the elation, then felt himself becoming mildly disappointed. *This can't be it.* There was so much more he wanted.

Then he heard, "Now, where was I? Ah, yes." Teague's head began its descent again down the middle of his chest, licking and suckling along the way. Key's abdominal muscles involuntarily spasming everywhere Teague's mouth touched, as it slid back and forth over the ridges of his abdominals, slowly licking and savoring, covering every inch of him. "Very nice. Ye are a beautiful man, laddie. And I see yer ardor hasn't diminished." His mouth descended on Key's ardor, taking him in, completely draining him.

Teague slid back up to capture Key's mouth yet again. Teague's hot lips burned his own. Key didn't think anything could be better.

But he was wrong. Teague's exploration showed him many new areas of his body which he never even knew were so sensitive... or maybe it was just the man himself who caused these feelings. Everywhere Teague's fingers, lips, and tongue touched was like a brand, searing his flesh with heat, making him Teague's eager possession.

"Would you like a turn now, laddie?" The words were whispered in his ear as if from far off. Key had been so lost in Teague's expert ministrations to his backside, he barely heard the words from the man who lay firmly on him. Key felt Teague's manhood firmly nestled between his buttocks, straining, tempting. He wanted more. Teague obliged, teasing with his hardness, causing Key to writhe, straining for satisfaction, heedless of the rough ground beneath him and the death of the flowers he was causing, his own hardness being the cause of many of their deaths. "Enough, laddie, there's plenty of time for that. I burn for yer touch." Teague's body slowly rolled off him, causing a shocking rush of coolness to cover Key's back, making him shiver. Key became aware of the scent of the flowers surrounding his head before he raised himself up, then turned to look upon the divine form of the man lying magnificently naked next to him, surrounded by heather and clover and buttercups.

Key could have stared at him forever. *This man was kissed by God.* Key hesitated, not knowing where to begin, only knowing that he had never wanted anything more.

"Do anything ye like, laddie. I'm all yers." Teague's head lay back on their pillowed clothing, arms at his sides, baring, tempting, seducing.

The words made Key's head spin with fantasy. *This must be a dream. An enchanted land... an enchanted man.*

"You have enchanted me," the Irishman murmured. "I must have ye, laddie." Teague held his arms up in supplication.

Key broke his spellbound stare and literally pounced on the Irishman. He wanted nothing more than to return the incredible pleasure that Teague had given him, and thereby giving himself the pleasure of enjoying this amazing man.

Key started by mimicking many of the techniques Teague had used, sending Teague into a fury of desire. Then, being caught up in his task, Key forsook mimicry and dove in wantonly with his own ideas. He could not get enough of the man, teasing his lower body with tongue and fingers, prolonging Teague's torture, before capturing the center of him, making him cry out in pleasure as Key himself had. Teague seemed to relish everything Key did to him, even encouraging his mouth and fingers in their exploration, nothing forbidden. Key did not hold back as his mouth worked in front, fingers probing in back, knowing the man's fulfillment was close.

"Ahh," Teague cried in release, clutching Key's head to him.

Key moved up Teague's body, meeting his lips and searing them to his own. "Now, we're even."

"Och, no, laddie. Not even a wee bit close. We are not nearly even." Teague took Key's mouth once again, rolling over on top of him, decimating another patch of heather.

A long while later, Key lay replete on Teague's sweat-soaked chest, nuzzling the hair there and idly playing with one of Teague's nipples, enjoying the afterglow, wishing it would never end. A very slight breeze cooled the sweat from his body. "Laddie, I know ye can see what you're doin' ta me. Are ye not sated yet?"

"I don't think I'll ever be," Key said honestly. "I could stay here forever."

Teague gave a sharp intake of breath, Then haltingly said, "Do ye mean that?"

"I... I think I might."

"I have very strong feelings for ye as well."

Key paused his fondling for a moment, and raised up to look into Teague's eyes. What he saw there, stunned him. Unfettered love. Key felt such a strong emotion well up in him that tears sprang to his eyes. Teague's look intensified and Key was lost. He lowered his mouth to Teague's and they became lost once more in one another.

They made love again as if it were the first time.

"Do you know what time it is?" Key asked, brushing the burnished mane of the wondrous man who lay upon his chest.

"Does it matter?" came the Irish lilt in response, his hand sliding up and down Key's torso.

"No... yes... I..." Key was torn. He never wanted to leave, yet he knew he had to. Bryan would be waiting. They needed to get back to... To what? He'd found what he was looking for. But he was young, twenty-one. Would Teague really want him? He was older— only by seven years, but still... He wanted to cry.

"Laddie, I know what ye're thinkin'." He rose up on one

elbow to look at Key. "I love ye. I love ye with every breath and bone in my body. I want to spend my life with ye."

Key's jaw hung open. *It's all too perfect. This is exactly what I wanted him to say. Something's not right, though. I know there's a 'but' coming.*

"But there is something ya need to know."

I knew it. Too perfect. "Tell me," Key managed to say.

"Ya need to hear it from me grandda. He'll tell ye the whole story. Then ye decide if ye want me or not." Teague face and demeanor took on a solemnity that frightened Key.

"All right. But you don't have a fatal disease or anything do you?" Key's voice had a vague manic tone to it.

"No, laddie. I'm fine." Teague smiled. "But ye need to know the truth about Cashel."

"Cashel?"

"Aye."

"Before I hear this story, I have to tell you something," Key said determinedly.

As he brushed Key's cheek, Teague said, "I'm all ears, laddie."

"I love you. And no story or town will change that. I know I'm younger than you are, but I know how I feel. I've never felt anything even close to this for anyone, so I know it must be love. The thought of not seeing you or not having you is unbearable to me. You've become part of me. I feel as if I'd die without you."

"That's love, laddie." Teague slowly brought his lips to Key's and kissed him so tenderly that Key felt he would faint from the love it conveyed.

Their lips parted. Key's eyes were immersed in Teague's. "Let's go hear the story."

✴ ✴ ✴

"I thought I'd be seein' ye lads a wee mite sooner than this," Teague's grandda said as they came through the door of the pub. "I'm guessin' Teague here was showin' ye the sights?" There was a genuine twinkle in his eye.

Key felt himself blush and averted his eyes from the old man.

"Ah, that's how it be between ye." The old man's eyes seemed to twinkle even more.

Key felt his face grow hotter.

"It's all right, macushlah. Ye need not be embarrassed." Teague grabbed Key's hand and squeezed it.

Key noted the Irish endearment.

"Nothin' to be embarrassed about, lad. My Teague's a fine man, he is. Now, get yerselves set on a stool here. We need to talk. And, as ye can see, I'm not right busy at the moment." He waved an arm indicating the empty bar. "And I think a draught might also be in order." The old man went to get their drinks.

They seated themselves at the bar, Key noting the lack of patronage, guessing the men of the village were out hard at work.

"Grandda, Key needs to know everything." Teague squeezed Key's hand again, not having relinquished his hold from before.

"Please, sir. It seems to be very important to Teague," Key said, enjoying the feel of holding hands with Teague.

"Lad, call me Paddy, as I'm thinkin' Teague here wants to keep ye around."

Another squeeze.

"All right, sir, Paddy it is." Key smiled at the old man.

Paddy went to the pour the beers, while Key contemplated his life, his future, Teague, and an ominous feeling beneath it all.

"Here ye are, lads." Paddy set down the beers for them and one for himself. "Slainte." He raised the metal stein, and Teague and Key joined the Irish toast.

Paddy took a long pull and began. "Several hundred years ago there was a brouhaha between our beloved St. Patrick and old scratch himself—the Devil. Now, the Devil was residin' in a cave nearby, and Patrick, with God's assistance, had him banished from the area. The Devil got so mad he bit off a chunk of rock from the cave and spit it out right here—The Rock of Cashel, or The Devil's Bit."

It was almost the same story Key had told Bryan earlier. But he wanted to hear it from a true Irishman. Feeling somewhat more at ease, he settled back and prepared to hear the Cashel legend. He was sure the old man would have some new blarney to add to the tale that Key loved so well.

"Patrick, in his good old Irish way, and to spite the Devil a wee bit more, decided he would build a church here in Cashel, high atop the Golden Vale, from where all Ireland could be governed. Now, this angered the Devil to no end, and no matter how much he fussed and fumed and threatened, he could not stop Patrick from his mission. Patrick it seems was truly blessed by God and was one of His favorites, and consequently had His divine protection. The Devil, bein' the devil he is, since he couldn't stop Patrick, concocted a curse on all Cashel and its people—exceptin' of course for Patrick." Paddy paused to take a swig.

Key joined him in the draught, then said, "I didn't know the part about Patrick having divine protection."

"Aye, ye wouldn't. Very few know of it. But it's true nonetheless," Paddy averred.

Key couldn't help himself. "But it's just a legend."

"Ah, laddie, I wish it were so."

Key squirmed on the stool, disconcerted. *The old man's losin' it.*

"Please, Key, just listen... for me." Teague reached for his hand again and held it.

Key was oddly comforted. "All right... for you."

Paddy smiled at the two men and continued, "The curse was this: All inhabitants of Cashel must remain here or the village would vanish forever. Mind you, we could live out our lives, have bairns, grow old and die, but we could never leave."

Key smiled at the use of "bairns," the Irish word for children.

"But it doesn't end there. Patrick, bein' blessed, was himself immune to the curse and could leave Cashel as he saw fit. The rub was that he had fathered a son here, who was not immune to the curse. Patrick, then, in his own vengeance for the curse, confirmed the church a cathedral, and it became the seat of power here in

Ireland for centuries, when Brian Boru's last descendant, Murtaugh O'Brien, became the last High King."

Key wondered where this was all going but kept silent. This was not the blarney he was expecting.

Teague squeezed his hand. "Are ye all right, macushlah?"

Key nodded and awkwardly smiled at Teague. "Perhaps, another draught?"

"Whatever ye want."

Key read Teague's subtext and tried to smile again.

Paddy swiftly refilled their steins and continued his saga. "Patrick, of course, as is natural, passed away, God rest his soul, and the Devil tried countless times to destroy Cashel and the blood-born of Patrick."

"Then in 1647 it happened. Someone left the village—and not just anyone—but the direct descendant of Patrick himself. For whatever reason, the lad developed the wanderlust and deserted the village. This was the opportunity the Devil had been waiting for all these hundreds of years. His revenge. He sent two of his minions, the Earl of Inchquin and his brother, who they said was sent by Cromwell, but we all knew who they were sent by. They plundered the village. Then, one Sunday, when we were all at Mass, the brothers and their soldiers surrounded the cathedral and set it ablaze. All eight hundred village folk were lost."

Key had heard this part of the story, or a form of it, leaving out the Devil part. Still, it sobered him just thinking about the pitiful trapped villagers.

"Now, if ye'll recall the other part of the curse, if anyone ever left the village it would vanish forever. Well, it seems that because the one who left was a descendant of Patrick, the village didn't disappear but was put in a limbo—God's helpin' hand I suspect—all of the eight hundred souls, 799 without Patrick. I didn't mention it, but all St. Patrick's descendants are named Patrick. The Devil was outfoxed again and in his furor laid a second curse upon us: All would be trapped in limbo until the blood of Patrick was spilt and all eight hundred villagers were reunited. Then we could live out our lives and our souls could finally pass on to our just deserves. An awful curse indeed." Paddy finished his tale and followed it by finishing his draught. He stared at Key. "There ye have it, laddie. The true tale of Cashel."

Key felt a shiver, then found himself saying, "You said 'we' and 'our just deserves.' What do you mean? You sound like you're talking about yourselves." Key realized his voice held a manic tone.

"Aye, Key," this spoken softly by Teague.

"No. It's impossible. It's just a legend. I know the story. All that other stuff, the blood of Patrick, and the town in limbo, you just made it up." He got up from the stool and began to pace around the bar. "You all died, burned up!"

"God saved us as best he could," Paddy said. "But the Devil is very powerful. We are now, all of us, in a limbo. We wake and we work and we sleep. We never get older. We never get sick. We never die. It's an empty existence. Nothing changes day to day. Any work we do has to be done again the next day, as if yesterday never happened. But—and this is the hardest part for us all—we remember. We know what we did the day before and know we have to do it all over again. Why do ye think I have so many customers early in the morning? They're tryin' to forget what's to come. But it doesna' work."

Key listened, but could not stop his pacing.

"Key... macushlah. Please, sit down. I know it's difficult to believe, but I want ye to try. I didn't mean to hurt ye by hearin' this. I never would. But ye had to know the truth. And it is the truth. I swear."

Key froze. Looked around. The pub. The people. Their clothing. The village. It did all seem like it was from another time. *Could it be true? The Devil? St. Patrick?* He tried to think rationally. There was no rationality here. *They say legends do have some basis in truth. But* this *much truth?* He slowly turned and looked at Teague. Teague's open anguish tore his heart apart as he watched the tears falling down the handsome man's cheeks. The look in his eyes, one of desperation and, still... love. He ran to Teague and held him. Teague began to sob in his arms.

"I love you so much," came Teague's choked voice. "I canna lose ye." He clutched Key harder. "Please... please... try... just try to believe. I swear on my love for ye, it's all true."

Key couldn't help it. He believed him. As his mind worked, piecing things together, he worked it through. He pulled Teague's tear-stained face off his chest and looked into those beautiful, water-filled emerald eyes. "I believe you."

Tears began to flow again from Teague's eyes this time from relief... and joy. He pulled Key to him and kissed him as if he never wanted to stop.

"Ahem." Paddy made his presence known.

Key and Teague slowly parted their lips, neither embarrassed in the least.

"Now that ye've accepted the truth, there is a wee bit more."

"All right," Key said. "In for a penny—" He stood between Teague's legs, one hand around his neck and waited for the old man to speak.

"Ye and yer friend are the first people to visit here since the curse was laid," Paddy said. "One of ye is the descendant of our St. Patrick."

"How could that be?" Key stepped away from Teague, who drew him back in.

"Only one of the Blood could have returned here. It's the only way to break the curse. But neither of ye is named Patrick."

Key's mind began to reel, his legs buckled, and Teague grabbed him to hold him up.

Key, macushlah, what is it? Speak to me." Teague's voice held genuine panic.

Key tried to formulate the words. "I–I'm... Patrick." He looked at Teague with fear in his eyes.

"Don't be afraid. I knew it," Teague said.

"And yer father?" Paddy prompted.

Key nodded. "He's–he's dead. So is my mother, a few years

ago, an accident."

Teague pulled him close.

"His name was Thomas—well, his middle name—but his first name, like mine, was Patrick." Key tried to focus. His grandfather, too. I hadn't thought about it in years. I never even remember *my* real first name is Patrick." Key felt dizzy. "Teague this is too much. What am I supposed to do now?"

"Laddie, stay calm. Ye are here for a reason. God led ye here. Perhaps, another wee draught will help calm ye," Paddy said and hurried to fill their steins.

"What reason?" Key tried to calm himself and think. "Why me?" He had a sudden thought. "And what about Bryan... and those *fucking* twins? Who the hell are they anyway? Is he all right?" His voice rose again. "Help me! I'm so lost." He collapsed into Teague's arms and began to cry, something he hadn't done since his parents' deaths. And with no siblings, he had never felt more alone.

"Ah my love, all will be fine. I swear it to ye. This is too much for any man. Ye go ahead and cry. I'm here for ye. I will always be." Teague held Key and rocked him gently. "Where are those bloody beers?" he snapped at Paddy.

In an instant they appeared. Teague held one to Key's lips as his tears subsided. Key drank. Then drank some more. "That's my lad," Teague said, squeezing him firmly.

"Well, if ye're wantin' to know my theory, this is it." Paddy was in raconteur mode again. "The, I believe ye said, *fucking*, twins, which is probably what they are doin' now with yer friend, are none other than the evil Earl of Inchquin and his brother. They are not part of our village, but I'm certain they are here to keep the curse from ever bein' broken. They are mere extensions of the Devil hisself. I know they tried seducin' ye and yer friend. They can become whatever they need to be. Yer friend wanted two virile men, and that's what he got. Ye were smarter, laddie. Ye knew there was somethin' not right about them. And ye were right." He paused, more for effect than because he needed to, Key thought. "Are ye still with me, lad?"

"Aye," Key mumbled, aiding the storytelling.

"Now, I'm sure, as the day is long, that they plan to keep ye both here. Since my Teague here swept you away from the evil-doers, they needed another plan. With the both of ye here, there are now 801 people—one more than the original 800. And I'm sure the Devil, in his way, has prescripted it so. Curses are an exacting thing. Every word is carefully selected. The curse says that when the 800, no more, no less, are returned and when the blood of Patrick has been spilt, the curse will be broken. As ye, Key, are the blood of St. Patrick, ye can fill the place, but more concerned am I about the blood bein' spilt."

"I can help ye there, Grandda. Blood was spilt. Key here cracked his head on the altar of St. Patrick and his blood flowed on it. The blood of Patrick was spilt. I'm sure it's how he came to be here. Am I right, Key?"

"I don't know. I guess it's possible. It seems anything is." Key was still so confused. His head ached. "I did see the way here through the mist after I cracked my head. So, maybe it's true."

"Ahhhh." Paddy drew out the word as if the secrets of the universe had just become apparent to him.

Suddenly, Key bolted upright. "I need to find Bryan. Teague, do you know where he is?" Key clutched his arms.

"I believe so, my love. We do need to find him before it's too late."

"What do you mean, 'too late'? They wouldn't hurt him, would they? I know Bryan may have his faults, but he's still my friend. If something's happened to him, I'll never forgive myself. I'm the one who dragged him here." He started to choke up.

Teague replied, "We'll find him. I promise. Don't ye fret. They need him." Then, almost to himself, he said, "If ye decide to stay with me, they need to keep him here as well."

Key stared at him, not knowing what to say, only knowing he had to save Bryan. "Show me where they've taken him."

* * *

They approached a large, rather dilapidated looking building. Key thought it might be a barn. "He's in there?" His voice held alarm.

"That's my guess," Teague said, portentously.

"How do you know?" Key was becoming agitated at the thought of what could be happening in the wooden structure.

"It's been used before," Teague flatly answered.

As they opened one of the massive doors, Key uttered, "Please let him be all right."

"Have courage." Key heard from Teague, which, coming from anyone else, would have sounded phony. It gave him strength.

"Bryan?" Key called to the darkened space. A little louder. "Bryan? Are you here? Teague, try over there. I'll go this way." He took a few steps, then thought he heard a faint groan from the other side of the barn-like building. "Bryan, it's me, Key. And Teague. We're here to help you. To take you out of here."

"He doesn't need help," a dark voice said. Then, appearing as if from nowhere, was one of the twins. Key couldn't tell which. And just as mysteriously, at his side appeared the other twin. Both naked. Both incredibly tumescent. "Have you come to join us?" the second one said. "We're ready for you." He wiggled his hips making his enormous erection flounce back and forth.

"Yes, *all* ready for you." The first wagged his hips similarly. Yet, in spite of their perfect physiques, the pair appeared cartoonishly grotesque to Key, their impossibly large organs swaying now in a disturbing synchronicity, their smiles matching rictuses of licentiousness. The twins' eyes locked on Key's, hypnotizing him. They reached for each other's swollen penises and drew themselves together and began kissing and stroking one another. Key tried to look away from the obscenity playing before him. He wanted to flee in revulsion, but was transfixed by their erotic performance. They seemed to slowly spiral, as if suspended by an invisible thread, their hands insidiously exploring backs and buttocks, chests and genitals.

Not wanting to be aroused, Key felt himself swelling with desire. His eyes frozen open, he began to rock in an unknown rhythm with the vertiginous display.

A voice broke the spell...

"He doesn't want anything ye two miscreants have to offer. He's mine. And we're taking Bryan with us." Teague stepped boldly from the dark, appearing almost as mysteriously as the twins had. "Take yerselves and yer ridiculous penises back to the hell ye were spawned from."

The twins hissed, or at least that's what Key thought it sounded like. Teague advanced, grabbing Key's hand, and the twins backed away into the shadows.

As they approached the far side of the building, the groaning got louder. Then Key heard, weakly, "Key? Key?"

"We're here," Key said. And two more steps brought them to where Bryan hung. He was naked, both arms tied over his head, legs fastened somehow with ropes to wooden crates, splaying them apart. Red welts oozed from his chest and abdomen. His genitals had a ring-type piece around them and a large stone hung suspended from it. As he got close, Key could see bruises everywhere: face, arms, thighs. Circling his suspended friend, Key cringed in horror. Back and buttocks raw from what could only be lashing of some kind. Then, Key noticed a trail of blood seeping from Bryan's anus.

He'd been raped and tortured.

Key's eyes filled. "Oh Bryan, this is all my fault. I'm so sorry." He glanced around and noticed, laying on the ground behind the boxes, the instruments of torture: a flail, some kind of pincers, a tool that looked like a cattle prod, which Key was sure had caused the rectal bleeding, a rope, and a whip. Key started to retch, the thought of the inflictions more than he could stand.

"Help me," Bryan's forlorn plea came.

Key stifled his heaving and said, "You're going to be all right, Bryan. Teague, I'll stand on the crate and hold him. You release his hands, then his feet."

Teague leapt to comply, standing on one crate and releasing first one arm then the other, while Key held Bryan from collapsing. Each arm being released brought a groan of pain from his friend, going straight to Key's heart. After untying both feet, Teague helped Key ease Bryan down to the floor of the barn.

"See if you can find his clothes," Key said, while cradling a fetal Bryan.

"I thought I saw them as we walked over here," Teague said, retracing their steps. "Here they are." He approached, holding some tatters of what used to be Bryan's T-shirt and jeans. "These are useless." He indicated Bryan's remnant of underwear. "But these will probably cover his modesty enough." He held up a pair of severely shredded jeans, now basically shorts with rips everywhere. "And I don't think he'll be wantin' to wear any kind of shirt for a while."

Key's voice was thick with emotion. "No, I don't think so. Are his sneakers here?"

"Ye mean these?" Teague held up Bryan's tennis shoes, which appeared to have fared better than the rest of his apparel.

They dressed Bryan as best they could. "You take one shoulder, I'll take the other," Key instructed. "Can you walk at all, Bry?"

Bryan, who had become somewhat more coherent, said, "I'll try."

Placing one of Bryan's arms over each of their shoulders, Key and Teague shouldered on. The twins had disappeared as mysteriously as they'd appeared. Key knew he hadn't seen the last of them.

After a few steps, Bryan choked out, "Be careful what you wish for." He sobbed. "I'm sorry, Key. So sorry. I love you, you know that, right?"

"I know, Bry. I love you, too. Don't talk. Save your strength. I'll get you home." He glanced at Teague, noticing his set jaw, and the fact that he would not meet his gaze. *Now what do I do? I'm totally fucked.*

* * *

They arrived back at the pub an hour later, the sun already setting. The bar was empty.

"This way." Paddy motioned the men to him. They approached a wall. "In here," he said. He miraculously pulled open a panel and a small room appeared, complete with two cot-type beds, a couple of metal basins, and a small table. Key wondered how the old man had conjured this up, then stopped his thought. *Nothing surprises me now.*

"Ease him down here. Paddy indicated the cot closest to the door. "There are some cloths and salves for his wounds. I use the room on occasion for some of my more neezled customers."

How had he known? Key wondered, slinking Bryan down onto the cot, hearing only a mild groan from his friend.

"These balms will help heal, and I have a draught for sleeping. He'll be much better come mornin'." Paddy glanced at Teague. "As ye may have noticed, I've closed for the evenin'. But I'm thinkin' ye two could use a draught or two and maybe somethin' a wee mite stronger. Teague help Key here with what to do with the salves and balms, then leave the lad to rest and heal. He'll be a sight much better come the mornin', I vow."

Teague knelt and did the applying, while Key gently held Bryan and whispered words of assurance.

Closing the door panel, Key said, "Thank you, Teague. For everything. Bryan could have died." His throat closed. Teague encircled him with his body.

"Macushlah, he wouldna have died. As my wise old Grandda Patrick here said, the fuckin' twins need Bryan to keep the curse in place."

They sat once more at the bar, drinks at the ready. This time, however, there was a smaller flagon beside the larger stein with an amber liquid inside. "Just what your barkeep prescribes," Paddy joked.

Key knew he needed something. He raised the flagon.

"Slainte."

"Slainte." The other two said, Paddy apparently having his own flagon at the ready also.

Key downed the liquor, feeling the heat course all the way down to his stomach. "Whew. I'm thinking that'll finally put hair on my chest."

"Ye don't need any, laddie. Ye're perfect as ye are." Teague's eyes smoldered at Key.

"Patrick Teague McLaren! I may be yer grandda, but some things need to be kept for private," Paddy chided.

Teague laughed. "I love this man, Grandda, and I love ye, ye old cur. And I would tell the whole bloody world if I could." He grabbed Key to him and branded him with a kiss.

"Ah, Teague me lad, I've waited many a year to hear ye say that." He stopped abruptly and turned away for a moment. Then he snuffled and turned back, eyes glistening. "Yer da would be so proud of ye."

Key stopped in mid-gulp. "Your da? Where is he? Is he here? Is he dead?"

Teague began, "Key, there is one other thing ye need to know."

Key sensed the change of mood. "Wait!" Key yelled. "Patrick. He called you Patrick. Patrick Teague McLaren. And *you.*" He pointed at Paddy. "You're Paddy. Patrick." He jerked back to Teague. "Who *is* your father? *Tell me.*" He slammed the stein down on the bar, beer spewing everywhere.

Teague sighed. "Me da is the man who left the village, never to return." Teague's face had a beleaguered look. "Aye. Me. Me da. Me grandda. We are all Patricks... like you."

Key took in this new information, and as it nurtured in his mind, his horror grew. "Your father is my... my... I don't know... great-great-great-great-*grandfather*? It can't be. I... we... we *can't* be. It's not right. It's impossible." Key bolted from the stool, went to the hidden panel, grabbed it open, and slammed it shut, not thinking about the recumbent Bryan, only feeling the need to get away. As the panel shut Key heard, "Don't, Teague. Leave the lad be. It's his decision now."

✷ ✷ ✷

Key opened the panel on a deserted bar. From the light coming in through the occluded windows, he knew it was morning, or daytime; he wasn't sure how long he'd slept. The bar was empty. *Where are they? Where's Teague?* Key's throat spasmed. The back door opened.

Their eyes met.

"I was just out back," Teague's halting voice said.

Key nodded. "I need to do the same." He walked toward Teague, eyes still locked. Then, passing him at the door, he breathed in the smell of liquor mixed with Teague's sweat. As he opened the door, he heard, "I'll wait here for ye." Key felt an underlying meaning of more than just a few minutes.

Key relieved himself in the outhouse, his thoughts so muddled he didn't notice the pungent aroma surrounding him. He zipped up and prepared himself for the conversation and decision of his future... and life.

He opened the door to the pub. There he was. Apparently, Teague was true to his word and had remained exactly where Key had left him.

Their eyes met again. Teague's held a combination of hope and despair. Key was devastated, knowing he had caused the pain in Teague's eyes.

Teague slowly raised outstretched arms to him in entreaty. Key couldn't resist. He stepped into Teague and let himself be enfolded, as his own arms came up to enfold Teague. Key breathed in the scent and basked in the warmth and firm pressure from the strong arms he so loved.

"Ah, macushlah, I..."

"Don't. Don't say anything. Just hold me. I need this one last time." Key took a deep breath, as he felt Teague's body stiffen at his words and give a quick intake of breath.

"I have to go," Key said into Teague's muscled chest.

Teague was stone. And silent. Key pressed his cheek to his chest and listened to the ever increasing beating of his heart. *How can I do this to him? Or to me?*

"This is all too much. And so much seems wrong. I can't seem to figure it out." Key hoped he didn't sound like a querulous school girl—even if that was how he felt.

Then Teague's hand came up to stroke his brow. Teague's lips brushed his ear and he said, "But do ye love me?"

Key knew he had to answer. "I thought I did. But I don't know if I can—or should." He pushed back from Teague and met his gaze. "But besides that, there's Bryan. Teague, he almost *died*. And it's my fault. I never should have let him go off with... *Them*." Even now bile came to the back of his throat at the thought of their cruelty. "I have to get him home. I have to. It's the least I can do. He needs to heal—and not just physically, although he seems to be amazingly better already, thanks to Paddy's remedies. I think he can make it back with my help. He needs to get away from here as quickly as possible; he needs to forget all this. And I know he'd never believe what's truly going on here. I barely do."

He knew he was rambling, but he had to get it all out before he changed his mind, or let Teague change it for him. He finished by saying, "And... and I need to get away. I need time to think. So much has happened. We can't really know if we love each other. It's only been one day. One *day*." Key stopped. He'd said too much. The look in Teague's eyes spoke volumes. *He does love me. Oh my God, how I've hurt him. This wasn't supposed to happen. I'll never forgive myself. I'm hurting everyone I care about. Including myself.* He couldn't take it anymore. That look. He pulled Teague to him, anything, so he wouldn't have to see the anguish in those emerald eyes. *How can I hurt someone that I love so much? Yes,* he admitted. *I love him.*

Teague spoke very slowly, "Ye're right, laddie. Ye need to go. Bryan needs ye. Ye go to him. Take care of him." He pushed Key away and nudged him to the paneled door. "Go. Please. It's for the best."

Key heard the agony in the Irish lilt, as he slowly walked to the door. He felt the searing stare of those emerald eyes following his very step. At the door, he stopped. He couldn't help himself. He looked back. Then he heard the final words...

"Promise me one thing, macushlah. In the years to come, ye'll find a moment or two to spare a kind thought of me."

Key yanked the panel open and flew into the room, needing to escape as the tears burst forth.

* * *

"Hey there, pal, what's wrong?" Bryan was sitting up on the cot, appearing to be far from death's door.

Key collapsed next to Bryan, and his big friend held him to him. "Oww," Bryan exclaimed. "Be a little careful. I'm pretty sore." He eased Key off him some. "But go ahead and cry. I know you feel sorry for me, but I'll get better, you'll see."

Key sobbed harder.

Bryan let Key cry himself out, not saying anything else, and in a few minutes Key was down to sniffles.

Key wiped his eyes. "I'm so sorry, Bry. It's all my fault. I never should have let you..."

"Wait a minute. It's not your fault. I made the decision. Well, both my heads made the decision. Maybe next time I'll let the bigger one, not *much* bigger, mind you, decide."

Key was puzzled by Bryan's tone. "Do you remember what happened, Bry? What they did to you?"

"Ah, you want the gory details, do you? Well, sure I remember. The twins, Dev and Luc, took me back to their place. It was like a big open place... I think. They asked me what I wanted to do, and I said, "I'm up for anything. And I was." He stopped.

"And?" Key prodded.

"Let me think. I was drinking a lot. And they gave me a flask of something on the way there, which was pretty potent. Oh yeah, they asked me if I liked to get tied up. I think I said yes. I'm pretty sure they did. And the way they looked naked— Whoa! Huge! *That* I remember."

Key cringed at the memory of those disgustingly large penises.

"Anyway, it was awesome. But I must have fallen down or something, maybe in some briar patch. I'm pretty achy and there are some red marks on me." He touched his chest tenderly. "Yep, still a little sore. But let's get going. I'll tell you more dirty details on the way home."

He doesn't remember. Thank you, God. At least something good has happened from this.

"Hand me my backpack. I can't seem to find my shirt. Guess I'll have to wear your blood-stained one. These jeans'll have to do." He held up the tattered clothing. "Those briars did a job on these. They might just cover the goods, since I seem to have lost my briefs, too. Whew, wild time." He started to stand. "Ow. Can you help me up a little, my legs and butt must've got a real workout."

Again Key cringed, recalling Bryan's bloody backside, as he helped him stand, letting the blanket fall away to reveal his nakedness. Let me lean on you while I get my shorts on. It's not like you haven't seen it all before." He looked down. "Is that a ring around my dick?"

Key looked down. More evidence.

"Yep. A good time." Bryan chuckled.

"Let's just go."

"You in a hurry? Hey, what happened with that guy you went to see the sights with? What was his name? He was pretty hot, too. Did you hook up?"

"Teague," he managed to say without choking up. "Teague. He showed me around. It was nice. Let's go."

"I think there's more to this story. The way he looked at you... Yeah, I know there's something you're not telling me."

"Maybe later, Bry. I can't right now."

"I get it, pal." Bryan said, his tone serious. "Look at me, Key." Key looked up from zipping Bryan's jeans. "I know I can be an egotistic prick sometimes, but I love you. I want you to know that I'm here for you. I'll do anything for you. And if you want to talk about it, I'll listen. You're a fantastic guy and my best friend. I want you to be happy."

It was almost too much for Key to take in. He wanted to bawl all over again. He wanted to tell Bryan everything. Maybe he'd believe it. But now was not the time. Maybe someday. "Thank you, Bry."

"Anytime. I mean it." Bryan stiffly bent to grab his backpack.

"I'll take it," Key said, relieving Bryan of the burden.

"Thanks, pal."

Key opened the door.

The bar was empty. No customers. No Paddy. No Teague. Key's heart broke yet again.

* * *

"I can't stand it anymore. You've changed, Key. That's all you do is mope around. You don't want to do anything. You dropped out of grad school. You don't date. Hell, I bet you don't even have sex! Do you at least masturbate?" Bryan chided from the barstool next to Key. He took a swig of beer. "Ever since we got back from Ireland. It's been months now. I mean it, you've got to do something."

"I'm fine," Key lied. "It's just, you know, I'm kinda blah. Grad school was boring. I need a career, I know. I can't survive forever on my parents' life insurance. And these guys around here are all the same. Nobody's serious. That's all they want is one night."

"Finish your beer. We need to have a heart-to-heart. Come on, over there." Bryan indicated a quiet table in the corner of the bar. He signaled the bartender for two more beers and they went to the table.

They sat down and the beers followed momentarily. "Bryan,

I've already had three." Key picked up the new beer and took a sip, in spite of his protestation.

"And we'll probably have a few more. Keep 'em coming," Bryan yelled to the back of the departing waiter. "We can stagger the couple of blocks home. That's the nice thing about living near you favorite neighborhood gay bar. And who wants to drive in Boston anyway—bunch of one-way streets all going the wrong way. I'm sure it was some drunk Irishman who engineered the whole mess. Which leads me to tonight's topic, or rather confession—yours."

Key stared uncomfortably at Bryan.

"Ireland. You said you were going to tell me and you haven't. We'll tonight's the night: Key's tell-all. What the fuck happened to you over there? I miss my friend. We live together, yet I don't feel like you're there. Something happened. You changed, and I'm pretty sure it's all about that hot Irish guy Teague. See, I remember his name. Come on, you owe me."

Key did owe him. But how could he tell him? He'd never believe such a fantastic tale. After all these months, Key wondered if he believed it himself. *Okay. Why not tell him?* Maybe Bryan would think him crazy, but he owed him some explanation for his behavior. "Finish your beer and order another. You're going to need it. A couple shots, too."

"That's my Key." Bryan motioned the waiter over. "Two more brews and two shots of your best Irish whiskey."

Over the next two hours, many beers, and several shots, Key told his story, trying to recount the legend/truth in his best Paddy, the raconteur, manner. The alcohol helped his confidence and he even dared the occasional Irish brogue for dramatic effect.

He didn't need to add any drama. Bryan was totally rapt. He said very little, only the frequent looks of astonishment and wonder gave any indication of what he was hearing. His only gestures were signaling another round to the waiter, who intuitively left them alone, only appearing to deliver their libations without uttering a word.

Key found himself caught in up in his account, realizing after a while that Bryan was not gainsaying a word. He related making love with Teague—with more explicit details than he'd meant to—but Bryan didn't add any of his usual crude commentary. He... listened, nodded, smiled, even got teary several times. Key found himself thinking: *This was a Bryan to love.* The only part of his recounting Key expurgated was Bryan's encounter with the twins. Since Bryan had still not remembered the actuality of the events from his encounter with them, Key was not going to tell him. Not ever. Let Bryan think he'd had the sexual fantasy of a lifetime. He owed him that much.

"...and I left Teague with that awful devastated look on his face," Key concluded. "It haunts me every day, and those last words, 'spare a kind thought of me.' If you'd heard the anguish in his voice..."

Bryan finally spoke. "You know what I think?"

"I can only imagine. I can't believe you really listened. You can run away anytime now." Key finished off his current beer.

"I think... you're an even *bigger* asshole than I am. I have a few questions, but *what were you thinking?* You walked away from Mr.

Perfect? For what? For me? I don't think so. And if you did, you're an even *bigger* asshole than I already think you are."

"What? Wait. You believe me?" Key was incredulous.

"Of course. I've known you a long time. You've never lied. Why would you start now? It certainly explains a lot things—like two hot twins just happening to be there ready to pounce on us for one. The weird looking bar, the clothes, the outhouse."

Key thought Bryan sounded surprisingly sober. As a matter of fact, Key felt surprisingly sober himself. Maybe it was the adrenalin from recounting everything to Bryan. "You're amazing."

"I know. Now, answer me some questions. How come your last name isn't McLaren?"

"I guess my great-great-whatever-grandfather changed it when he left Cashel so no one could find him. It's only a guess. We'll probably never know. Are you drunk?"

"I don't think so. Next question. If you go back, it'll be like you hardly left, since they're frozen in time, sort of. Therefore, it'll be like the next day over there. And by you staying there, you'll break the curse. Everyone lives out their lives, including you. And the town—I guess—vanishes, because it exists on a different plane or dimension." Bryan nodded his head in affirmation to his deductions. "Oh sorry, I guess that wasn't really a question. Here's one. Why do you think it's wrong to love Teague? Over four hundred years have gone by. It's not like you hooked up with your father."

"I know. I realize now I was stupid. It just shocked me, being related, sort of, and all. I think I'm starting to feel those shots." Key put his head in hands and leaned on the table.

"You're not using that as an excuse. Next question. Are you in love with him, and could you live with him for the rest of your life? I guess that's two questions. Look at me." Bryan grabbed Key's face and turned it up to meet him.

"Yes. To both," he said without hesitation.

"Like I said... *ass-hole*. You're miserable, Key. You love him and can't live without him. There's nothing for you here. You don't want to do anything. You're not interested in anyone. You need to go back. Now." Bryan shook Key's head to convince him, causing a slight groan from Key.

"But, you..."

"Key, you'll always be my best friend, and as *your* best friend, the best-friendliest thing I can do is let you go and be happy. I know you'd do it for me. Besides," he paused, "I think I might be ready for a real relationship. I know it's a shocker, but there's this guy at the gym I've kinda been seeing. I didn't tell you, 'cause I wasn't sure. He's smart. He's hot. And he's really into me. He's sees past my outer beauty and really *likes* me. I'm gonna give it a shot. I've had so much random sex, it's kind of lost its appeal. But sex with someone you care about is different, I've discovered. It's fulfilling, which in its way makes it even hotter. Chad, that's his name. Twenty-six. Owns four gyms already and is opening two more. He's already mentioned he can't handle it all and more than hinted at me being a partner. So, you see. I'll be fine. You... will not be. Not unless you get your ass on a plane a.s.a.p., my friend."

Key stared at the *new* Bryan. *When did this happen? A boyfriend? How did I miss it?* Then he realized. *I've been so self-absorbed, I didn't see anything going on around me. But what changed him?* The second realization hit him. The rape. Even if Bryan said he didn't remember it, on a subconscious level he must have. *Maybe some good did come out of it.* "I'm very happy for you, Bry. I'd love to meet him."

"Too bad you have to leave, I would have liked you to. We'll get your plane ticket when we get home. I'll close your accounts for you and turn the money over to me. Maybe I'll help finance Chad's next couple of gyms. We'll see how it goes. Besides, you won't need it. You couldn't even use it there. They probably don't even know what *America* is, let alone money." Bryan raised his hand. The drinks magically appeared. "One last toast to celebrate our futures. Slainte."

Key's decision, the only one he could—or wanted to—make, was made. And it took Bryan to help him see it. An image formed in his mind: Teague. He felt a rush of excitement and joy. "Thank you, Bry. Slainte."

* * *

The Rock of Cashel was covered in mist. It was morning. Key stood before St. Patrick's cross. Terrified. Where was the opening in the mist? Where was Cashel? Where was Teague?

He waited.

Nothing. Fog everywhere, thicker than the last time he was here. Maybe it would take a little longer because of it. Maybe he wasn't really a blood descendant of St. Patrick.

Blood. He remembered. "When the blood of St. Patrick is spilt." That's how the opening had appeared before. When he'd fallen and cut his head on the pedestal. "Bryan," he said aloud, "If it wasn't for you, none of it would have happened. If you hadn't pushed me..."

Would it work again? He had to try. He took off the backpack he'd been carrying, the one that contained all his worldly possessions he'd wanted to take. There wasn't much. But he had brought some modern conveniences he thought might be useful—like a Swiss Army Knife. He reached in the side pouch and pulled it out. He'd bought it in Dublin at the last minute, before hopping the bus here. He'd thought all the tools on it might come in handy.

"Well, here goes." He opened the blade and chose the middle finger of his left hand. "It's the biggest, so more blood." He drew in breath and cut the tip. "Ouch." The blood oozed forth. He held his hand over the altar. The blood slowly dripped. He squeezed his finger some to make it flow faster. He hoped it was enough. He smeared the blood around on the stone, then put his finger in his mouth and sucked on it.

He held his breath.

Nothing.

Something.

Off to the right the mist started to get thinner, or maybe he was just hoping it was.

No. It was getting thinner. He walked toward it.

The tunnel opened up. "I did it." He raced through.

There it was. "Cashel," he whispered almost reverently. "Nothing's changed. You're exactly the same." Or so he hoped.

There was the pub, just as he'd left it. As he approached the door, his pace slowed. That terrifying feeling returned. "Is this for nothing? Do you still love me, Teague? You have to." With determination he opened the door.

The bar was crowded—at least fifteen people. He scanned the room, recognizing a couple of men. A few faces turned his way, then a few more. Uncomfortable, he took three or four steps into the bar—and stopped cold. There at the end of the bar...

The Twins.

They glared at him. Their hatred palpable.

"They can't hurt ye, laddie," came a voice at his side.

Key turned his head.

"Paddy!" Key threw his arms around the old man.

"Aye, laddie. I knew ye'd come back. Ye're a good lad." He hugged Key back. "And how is your Bryan?"

Key's throat closed a little. "He's fine. He's great. He's in love."

"I knew he'd find his way. And have ye found yers?" Paddy looked at him directly.

"I hope so. Where is he?"

"I dinna know. He wasna here when I opened. I believe he was a wee troubled and needed to be alone."

Key cast his eyes downward. "I *have* to see him. I have to tell him how sorry I am that I hurt him. I have to tell him how stupid I was. I have to tell him how much I love him." He started to choke up.

Paddy's eyes were misty. "Aye, laddie, that ye do."

"But where could he be?" Key stopped. "I know where he is."

"Then go to him, lad. Tell him."

* * *

Key ran up the hill.

At the top he looked out. Flowers as far as the eye could see. Dazzling shades of beauty, just as he'd pictured every day since he'd left.

Key walked down the hill to where he and Teague had made love. *He has to be here.*

Key approached the area of crushed flowers.

Teague.

There he was, lying curled up. With his back to Key, his shoulders slowly shook.

Key's heart broke. *I did this to him.*

The shaking stopped. Teague slowly turned over and in a raspy voice he said, "It canna be. Ye're not real." He rubbed his tear-stained eyes. "Key?"

"Aye."

"Have ye come back to me? Truly?" Teague rose up on one elbow.

"Aye," was all Key could choke out again.

Teague extended one arm up toward him.

Key rushed to him and held him as if he would vanish. "I'm so sorry. I was so wrong. You *have* to forgive me."

"Hush now, macushlah. There's nothin' to forgive. Ye did what ye thought was right. There was no wrong. Ye had to make yer own decision."

"I know, but I didn't mean to hurt you."

"Hurt comes with love. And the more we love, the more it hurts. And do ye love me, laddie? Are ye sure this is what you want?"

Key looked into those sparkling emerald eyes with those flecks of gold. "With all my heart. Forever."

"And I love ye with all *my* heart. Forever."

Key's heart filled joy. *This is right.*

Teague stood up and brought Key with him. "Now, are ye ready to break this curse and start our future?"

"Yes."

Teague brought his lips to Key's. "Then, macushlah, I say we break it with a kiss."

* * *

Up on the hill, early morning visitors had come to see the legendary Rock of Cashel and the famous cathedral of St Patrick. On this particular morning, visitors were gifted with the tintinnabulation of the ringing of the cathedral bells—from a cathedral tower that was no longer there.

VIRGO

Virgo-The Virgin

Traits: modest, reliable, intelligent, patient, kind, strong sense of moral and ethical conduct, critical, practical, a mutable quality that makes one adapt to change

He was battered, bloodied, and beautiful. The man standing in Jared's cabin doorway uttered one word, "Help," before he collapsed into Jared's arms. Jared looked out into the snow-covered forest and saw no other signs of life. How had this man gotten to his cabin up here in the desolation of the Rocky Mountains?

Several hours later, Jared sat staring into the angelic face of the man now quietly resting in his bed. It had been no mean feat dragging the dead weight of the quite solid form of the man through his house and into his bedroom. Jared was glad he had had a personal gym installed into his Colorado writer's retreat. He diligently spent an hour and a half each day with weights and cardio training, and he was happy with his looks. As a bestselling horror writer, he was sought out for many more television interviews and photo shoots than his peers because of his good looks. His agent and publicist were also quite happy that his dark, good looks and media exposure sold more books. *Take that Stephen King.* But he hadn't published a new book in two years, and his agent wasn't so pleased with him now. Jared certainly didn't need the money—ten New York Times bestsellers, the last four making it to number one—but he loved writing. His idyllic life had been shattered when that *prick* Brad came home one day after they'd been happily—or so he'd thought—married for twelve years and announced that he didn't love Jared anymore and was no longer attracted to him. It turned out that Brad had traded him in for a younger—by fifteen years—model than Brad. That trauma had put Jared into a depression for the past two years and he'd had no inspiration to write.

So, here he was in the middle of winter, in his writer's retreat: no phone, no radio, no television. And: no ideas, no career, no lover. He'd been here for two months, since just before Thanksgiving. His cabin, all four thousand square feet of it, was well-stocked with food enough for a long winter, but it was sparsely furnished. He'd outfitted the kitchen, living room, library/writing den, gym, and his bedroom, where he now sat on a chair, contemplating the man still quietly resting before him. Actually, the man was more of a boy. He couldn't be more than twenty-five. He had short, straight, honey-colored hair, and a strong, smooth, unlined face. Except for a chin abrasion and a small cut over his left eyebrow—Jared had cleaned the cut and wiped the dried blood away— his patient appeared unharmed. Of course, he had also had to remove the man's torn parka and clothes to check for other injuries. *What a body.* There had only been a slight discoloration on the man's right shoulder. Jared stared at it now, the sheet and blanket were lying just below a smooth and rather muscular chest.

Who was he? An angel dropped from heaven? A serial killer on the run?

Wait. An idea. A writer alone at his mountain retreat. The dead of winter. A storm. A possible serial killer? An attraction? Yes! It could work. It was kind of Misery-esque, but that dealt with a crazed female fan who was fat and ugly. But this guy—Jared looked at the resting man—*was gorgeous!*

And after all, Ted Bundy was hot. What about the gay angle? He'd always tried to push the envelope in his writing. *Yes. It could definitely work.* His fans would eat this one right up.

"Pretty." A hand touched Jared's face.

"*Aargh!*" Jared screamed and fell backward off the chair.

He was awake.

Jared scrambled for the chair and his composure. "Are you all right?"

"Hurts."

"Who are you?

Nothing.

"What's your name?"

"Don't... know... maybe... Dray?" His eyes closed.

"Dray?" *Interesting. It should have been Adonis.* "Do you remember what happened to you?"

Nothing. He was asleep again.

Jared decided to grab his laptop and start writing down his new book idea. "I might as well utilize my time until you, Dray, decide to wake up again," he said to the recumbent man. At least it seemed like his house guest was going to live. But where had he come from?

* * *

Three hours later, and a chapter and a half into his new novel, Jared heard, "Thirsty." Two blue eyes—crystal blue—stared up at him. He reached for the glass he'd prepared for the man's eventual awakening and held it to Dray's lips. The young man drank greedily.

"Hold on there, Dray. Not too fast."

"Is... that my... name? Dray?

"That's what you said it was, about three hours ago."

"Where... am I?"

"You're in my cabin in the Rocky Mountains, and my name is Jared."

"Jared. Pretty man."

Jared felt himself blush. "Thank you," he mumbled. "Do you know how you got here? What happened to you?"

"No. Head hurts." His breathing became agitated. "Fire! Mother! *Nooo!*" Dray screamed and grabbed Jared's hand, his eyes looking straight up.

"It's all right, Dray. You're safe here with me." Jared put his other hand atop Dray's.

Dray visibly calmed. "Safe... Jared... pretty." And he fell asleep, still clutching Jared's hand.

Inexplicably, tears sprang to Jared's eyes. "You poor kid, I'll keep you safe," he said to the resting man.

At least now Jared knew there had probably been a plane crash, a fire, and a possible explosion. Were there other survivors? In this weather he couldn't go out and search. Snow had started falling several hours ago, and now it was a full-on blizzard. They—*they*— were snowbound.

Jared glanced at the fireplace to see if it needed stoking, but the blaze was burning strong and he had plenty of wood. The hand that still held his was strong and virile. Who was this perfect creature that thought he was... pretty? It seemed an odd word to be used by an adult, however young, but Jared found it charming. *Charming.* Ten words and he was falling for this guy. Well, it had been two years since he'd had... anything. Of course he was vulnerable. But this guy was just a kid, regardless of how perfect, and that could only spell trouble. He was forty-two, old enough to be this kid's father, or at least an older brother. *And, hello. Probably straight.* But he did say, "pretty."

* * *

Jared wrote for another hour, but it was slow going. He only had one hand, the other still locked in Dray's grasp.

"Well, Sleeping Beauty, I need some rest, too," Jared said to the silent form as he slowly eased his hand free. "Maybe this is why I never bothered to furnish the other bedrooms. I only have the one bed, so you'll just have to share. Besides, this will be better for *you,* in case you wake in the middle of the night and need something."

Dray didn't stir.

"Yeah, right! Better for *who?*" Jared undressed, pausing at his jockeys, deciding whether to keep them on or not. "What the hell, Dray. You're naked. I always sleep that way. Why change now?" He removed his briefs and realized he was more than a little aroused. He got into bed. "This is going to be a long night, Dray. Be gentle with me," he joked.

Silence answered him.

Jared reached over to turn off the bedside light and felt an arm fall across his midsection. Jared turned back quickly. "Hey, Dray..." Silence. He lay back down still under Dray's arm. The bed moved as Dray snuggled closer. "A *very* long night," Jared said to the ceiling and proceeded to count sheep.

* * *

Jared awoke from the most exquisitely erotic dream to find the subject of that dream still pressed close to him. It was morning, he guessed, but Dray still wasn't up, at least... awake up. With Dray glued to his body, one part, a very *large* part of him, was definitely awake. Jared had to get away. He slowly, if reluctantly, moved out from under Dray's arm. He stood and stretched in the cool air. The fire had gone out during the night. Maybe the air and a cold shower would help. He looked down at the cause of his discomfort. He looked around quickly for his underwear.

"You're naked."

Jared whirled around to the voice.

"And big."

Jared futilely tried to cover his crotch with his hands. He knew he looked ridiculous.

"Me too." Dray threw back the covers to reveal the truth of his words.

Jared's throat went totally dry and his mind became a vacuum. He was sure he knew some words in the English language, but right now he couldn't think of one.

"Are you okay? Your face looks funny." Dray rose from the bed.

Jared tried for a coherent thought.

Dray rose and took a step. His knees buckled; he clutched his head.

Nakedness forgotten, Jared rushed to Dray and grabbed him before he fell.

Dray grabbed onto Jared and held fast. "Dizzy." He pulled Jared closer, pressing his head into Jared's. They were the same height.

Jared held him and breathed in the musky, slightly smoky, scent of him. "It's all right, Dray. You just moved a little too fast. I'm right here. You'll be okay in a minute."

"I'm scared, Jared." Dray began to cry.

He knew he should probably find some clothes, but right now it didn't seem to be important. Dray seemed oblivious to their nudity, anyway. So Jared rubbed his head soothingly. "Shh. Shh. "Everything's going to be all right." He hoped.

"I like you." Sniffle. "You're nice." Sniffle. "And pretty."

"Thank you, Dray." What else could he say?

"You feel nice, too. And smell good." Dray was rubbing Jared's back now with one hand and fingering a bicep with the other.

Jared realized he was doing the same thing to Dray and

stopped, stiffening. "Perhaps you should lay back down on the bed till you feel better."

"I like you holding me. Don't you like to hold me?"

It was a simple question, with *oh* so complicated an answer. "Yes, I do."

"Good."

"Too much," Jared continued.

"You make me feel warm, and tingly and... I don't know. I feel... I want—"

"We can't," Jared said still not releasing him.

"Can't what?"

"You know." *Brilliant.* A writer, and the best he could come up with is 'you know.'

"Can't touch? But I like to touch you, Jared. You're all hard and muscley, and fuzzy on your chest. He rubbed his hand back and forth over Jared's sprinkling of chest hair.

Jared groaned.

"Did I hurt you?" Dray stopped his caress, real concern shown on his face.

"No. But it feels too good." Jared could feel the tension building in both of them, especially since their naked bodies were still connected everywhere. He had to stop this. "How old are you?"

"Thirty-three. How old are you?"

Thirty-three. Not a kid. A man. All man. Uh oh. "Forty-two."

"Oh."

Jared waited for more of a response and received none. How

could he be so innocent at thirty-three? Something wasn't adding up. "Have you ever had a girlfriend?"

Dray hesitated, furrowing his brow adorably. "I don't think so."

"A boyfriend?"

"I don't think so."

"A lover?" Jared held his breath.

Again. "I don't think so."

Jared expelled his breath, exasperated. "How can you not know?"

"Some things I can't remember. They're fuzzy."

"Do you remember what happened to you and how you got here?"

Dray did that adorable brow furrowing thing again. "No."

"Do you remember where you live? Do you have a family?"

"I... my mom... and dad... they..." Dray's face started to contort. "They..."

He screamed and pushed away from Jared. "Noooo!" Anguish.

Jared pulled Dray back into his arms. "Shh. Shh. Don't think about it. I'm right here. Just take deep breaths. That's it. Easy... easy."

Dray was sobbing hard into Jared's chest, clutching his shoulders for dear life.

"I don't wanna remember! Please! Please! Don't make me!"

His pleas broke Jared's heart. What had happened? Dray had screamed out, "Fire!" and "Mother!" *A plane crash? How horrible.* That would explain the bruising and abrasions. And the smoky smell. That type of trauma could certainly cause the partial amnesia Dray seemed to have. But there was more to Dray, he was sure. *How could he be so innocent and naïve? He was thirty-three years old!*

"It's all right, Dray. You don't have to remember. Lie down and rest for a while." He eased Dray down onto the bed. "You could probably use some food, too. You must be starving."

Dray sniffed and nodded. "I have oatmeal for breakfast. It's my favorite."

Jared smiled at him. "Mine, too. Oatmeal it is. Raisins, brown sugar, and cream?"

Dray gave Jared a breathtaking smile, seeming to have forgotten about the hysteria of moments ago.

Whoa. That smile could melt an iceberg. Jared knew he was in big trouble. He felt the stirrings of desire and realized that he was still naked. He scanned the floor for his briefs.

"Here." Dray handed Jared his briefs, seeming to have pulled them from midair. "But I think you look better without them," he said, guilelessly.

Jared groaned again and quickly donned his briefs to cover his growing excitement, not that it did much good. "You can help yourself to any of my clothes from the closet and dresser over there. Everything should fit. We're about the same size." *Everywhere.* Jared glanced down quickly at Dray. "I'll be back shortly." He should have thrown on a robe or something, but Dray had already seen it all so... *What the hell.* He could probably use the cooling off.

"Jared!" A blood-curdling scream.

Jared flew back to the bed. "Dray, what's wrong? Are you hurt?"

Dray's eyes filled with tears. "Can I come with you? I don't want to be alone."

Jared put one arm around his shoulder and hugged him. "Of course, if you feel up to it. I'll get you my robe."

"But it's yours," Dray protested.

"You take it. I'm a little warm." *Understatement.*

"Thank you," Dray said, a little shyly.

Good God!

* * *

They sat at the small breakfast table and ate.

"This is the best oatmeal I've ever had," Dray said.

Jared nodded. "It did come out pretty well. That touch of honey was a good idea."

"That's the way I always have it, Jared. Jared. I like your name." Breathtaking smile again.

Jared felt his face heat up. Again. "I like yours, too. I don't think I've ever heard it before. What's your last name?"

"I don't know. What's yours?"

"Crane."

"Jared Crane!" Awareness struck. "You write those spooky books. I've read them all, even though I'm not supposed to read them. You're much better looking than your picture on the backs of the books."

If he blushed one more time... Jared never blushed. What was up with him? "Why aren't you supposed to read them?"

"They're scary. But I sneak them out of our library. You're my favorite author."

No blushing! Wait! Favorite author... 'I'm your number one fan!' *Misery* again. Jared shook that thought aside. "Thank you. Did you know that my great-great-great—I can't remember how many greats—grandfather was Stephen Crane, who wrote—"

"The Red Badge of Courage. I didn't like it. It was boring. Even the battle scenes," Dray said, musingly. "Wouldn't you be scared if someone was firing a gun at you? Sometimes it's braver to run away. Henry Fleming felt too guilty. He was just scared. And then, to make up for running away, he tries to show everyone, and himself, how brave he is and gets into every battle he can. I didn't believe it."

"I agree," Jared said, enrapt. "It was supposed to be a realistic accounting... coming of age in the war, facing your fears, cowardice versus bravery, but it—"

"Was boring." Dray smiled, crystal-blue eyes twinkling.

Jared couldn't help laughing. "Yeah. You're quite the critic." He paused. *"I* started writing a new novel, while you were sleeping. You actually gave me the idea. I should dedicate it to you." Now why had he said that?

"Really? Jared. *Really?* Wow! That would be... would be..." Dray got up from the table and rushed over to Jared, engulfing him

in a bear hug.

That's why he'd said it—to give this very special man such unparalleled joy.

"I love you, Jared."

"What?" Jared said, warily.

"I love you. You take care of me and hold me and make the best oatmeal and... you wrote a book for me." Dray looked into Jared's eyes.

"Thank you, Dray." This was open honest love from one human being to another. A no-strings-attached, honest declaration. No guile. No ulterior motive. It was beautiful. And totally humbling. Jared was also starting to piece together a background for Dray: a sheltered life, simple in his thinking—but not dumb or slow, openly caring and loving, and maybe a little too trusting. He could be hurt very easily and his feelings ran deep. His parents, perhaps because of his open trusting nature, had tried to shelter him, to protect him from the harsh realities of life. Why? Who knows why parents do things to, or for, their children. But Jared feared that when Dray's memory did return, all hell would break loose, maybe scarring Dray permanently. Jared would do what he could for this poor innocent he was becoming way too involved with. He was starting to feel like Piper Laurie in that movie and novel, *Tim*. Except, he was the older man falling for the young, simple-minded, gorgeous hunk. Although, Jared would take Dray over Mel Gibson any day. He had to stop thinking like this.

Jared slowly extricated himself from Dray's arms. It felt too good. "It looks as if the weather is getting worse." He motioned to the kitchen window. "We won't be going anywhere for a while. Maybe if the snow lets up I can try to drive to town." Who was he kidding? That was seventy miles. It would be days, or perhaps weeks, before the road, such as it was, would be cleared enough for him to get out. There were drawbacks to seclusion. He had been warned to have some kind of communication device up here, but he'd refused. Maybe there was a reason for it. Fate was tricky. Dray needed help and Jared was the only game in town. Maybe they were fated to help one another. He'd already started writing again. Dray was inspiration. In many ways. Jared needed to take it slowly. This guy had partial amnesia and was probably a virgin. *Where had that come from?* They needed time to get to know one another before anything more could develop. Well, it looked like they would have it.

* * *

Jared and Dray spent the first part of the afternoon in the gym. Jared worked out. Dray was still not feeling up to activity like lifting weights and was content to sit and watch, which was a little disconcerting for Jared, who had hoped to work out some of his tension. Dray had made the occasional off-hand comment about Jared's muscles, or about a particular exercise he was doing, all seemingly innocent. Jared was the one who read more into the comments.

After the gym, they spent the rest of the afternoon listening to music and talking about books.

"I love to read any kind of horror or fantasy. I like to picture the different worlds and creatures. Sometimes I read romances too, when I want a happy ending," Dray said.

"Do you like horror movies?"

"I don't get to see many movies. But I like them."

More sheltering. "Well, I have a pretty good collection of movies I think you would like. I don't get any TV reception up here, but we can still watch DVDs. Maybe later?" Jared proposed. *With popcorn, snuggled up in front of the fireplace.* He had to stop these thoughts.

"Can we have popcorn and sit in front of the fireplace?"

Dear God!

"We'll see. I think maybe you should rest for a while now. You've had quite an ordeal. Sleep will help you to recover faster."

"Okay, Jared. Are you going to rest, too?"

"No. I think I'll write for a while." Jared jerked his head up. "Wow. It's been a long time since I've said that! It feels good."

"Why?"

"Well..." Jared struggled. "I didn't feel like writing anymore."

"Why?"

"I..." Jared committed. "What the hell. There was this guy—"

"He hurt you, didn't he." A statement not a question.

"Yes." Jared was open-mouthed.

"And it made you sad, and you didn't want to write any more stories, because writing stories made you happy, but you didn't want to be happy."

Jared was stunned. *Whew! This guy was perceptive.*

"But now you're happy again because I'm here, and so you want to write," Dray said simply.

"I'm not quite sure that's the reas— Yes, Dray, that's exactly why" And Jared knew it was true.

Dray smiled hugely. "Would you write in the bedroom while I nap, like yesterday?"

"Sure." Jared smiled back.

✳ ✳ ✳

Dray slept for several hours while Jared cranked out quite a few more pages. The words were coming quickly to him and he was excited. It felt great. And all thanks to the gorgeous sleeping— He glanced over to see two crystal blue eyes watching him.

"You make funny faces while you write."

"I do not!"

"Yes, you do. It's like reading the story on your face."

"Oh," Jared said, somewhat abashed. "I never had anyone watch me when I write before."

"Does it bother you?"

"No." Jared was surprised to discover that.

"Are you hungry? I am. I can make us something to eat. I'm good. Our cook says I am anyway."

"Cook?"

"At our house."

"Your house? You remember?"

"It was big." Dray's brow furrowed in that adorable way he had when he was thinking hard. "And Cook gave me lessons every day. Her name was Grace. She was nice."

"What else? What about your family? Your name—"

"Nope. That's it." Dray shook his head and threw off the covers. He was at least wearing underwear, Jared's, this time, which did little to deter Jared's imagination.

"Jared, come help me make dinner. It'll be fun."

"All right," Jared said, as if he could refuse. Then hurriedly added, "You can grab any shirt and pants you'd like. I'll just shut down my laptop."

* * *

In the kitchen, Dray was whipping up some vegetable pasta dish while Jared sat and admired how his T-shirt and favorite old pair of jeans fit Dray like a second skin. He hoped he wasn't drooling.

"All done," Dray announced, breaking Jared's erotic reverie. "Let's eat."

Ouch.

* * *

Dinner was delicious. Dray had a great sense for the combining of spices. What other hidden talents did he have?

After cleaning up the dishes, they sat in the living room and sipped Armagnac, Jared's favorite after dinner drink, and listened to "Kismet," his favorite musical.

"This burns my throat a little," Dray said, referring to the Armagnac, "but after you swallow it, it leaves a nice sweet taste in your mouth."

"An excellent description. And that's why it's my favorite." Jared held the snifter up to eye level and swirled it.

"This is your favorite music, too. I can see it in your face. You look happy, Jared."

Jared looked over at the man who had turned his world around and brought him back to life in just one day. "I am happy." The tenor on the recording sang:

Won't you answer the fervent prayer of this stranger in paradise,
Don't send me in dark despair, from all that I hunger for...

Dray smiled. "I like that song. The words are very beautiful."

Tears stood in Jared's eyes. "It's my favorite." He looked into the blue eyes of *his stranger.*

"Jared? Can I read your new book?"

That caught him off guard. "I never let anyone read my work till it's finished."

Dray was crestfallen. "Oh. Okay."

What a heartless jerk I am. Jared immediately recanted. "But I could make an exception. After all, you were my inspiration."

Dray was given the moon. "Can I read it now?" He jumped to his feet.

A huge lump in Jared's throat prevented him from responding. The unadulterated joy that flowed from Dray made Jared also feel as if *he'd* just been given the moon. "Finish your Armagnac and I'll print it out for you.

Dray tossed the drink back.

"You're supposed to sip it." Jared couldn't help but laugh. "Here let me refill our glasses and I'll turn on the printer."

"Hurry, Jared."

Jared grinned from ear to ear.

* * *

"Wow. The first *page* is creepy," Dray said not looking up. "You may have to hold me again tonight in bed, so I don't have nightmares."

Jared's throat seized up.

Dray looked up, a twinkle in his eye.

Was Dray flirting with him?

"I'm just kidding, Jared."

Jared's throat eased. A little.

"Scary stories don't give me nightmares." Dray returned to reading. "But I would like you to hold me anyway."

Jared's throat re-seized. His mind was awhirl. *It must be the Armagnac.* He shifted uncomfortably in his chair.

They had both finished their second and *third* Armagnacs by the time Dray finished the forty or so manuscript pages.

Dray looked up. "I really like it, Jared. It has a creepy but ordinary feel to it, which makes it all the scarier. Is the visitor really a serial killer? Is the writer in love with him? Please tell me."

"That's where I draw the line. I am *not* revealing the ending. And you can beg and plead all you want to, with those beautiful, crystal-blue eyes of yours—*Was that out loud?*—but I'm not going to tell you!" The liquor, or something, had gone to his head.

"Okay, Jared. But I think this is your best book."

"But you've only read a few pages."

"I can tell. The story jumps right off the page, like you're really there. Do you really think I'm handsome?"

Dammit. Dray had figured out the visitor character was modeled after him. What the hell. Tell him. "Yes, I do." Then added, "Very."

"I think you're handsome, too." Dray smiled. "Very."

Dray *was* flirting with him now. He was sure of it. *Maybe he's just drunk, too.* "I thought you said I was 'pretty.'"

"On the inside. Handsome is for a man on the outside."

Incredible.

Dray was still staring directly into Jared's eyes. "Do you want to go to bed now?"

Work, tongue! Work. Jared cleared his throat. "Are you tired?"

"A little. I think it's the Armagnac. I hope you have a lot of it, Jared. I think we should drink it every night after dinner."

Every night.

Dray continued, "I think I might be a little drunk, too, Jared.

I don't get to drink alcohol much."

"Well, if it's any consolation," Jared laughed nervously, "I think the Armagnac went to my head, too." *Or you did.*

They went to the bedroom.

"Tomorrow I'll just be quiet and sit and read a book all day, so you can write," Dray said as he stripped off his T-shirt. "Can we sleep naked again, Jared?"

Jared froze with his shirt halfway over his head.

"I like the way your body feels next to mine."

"Jared stared at Dray's muscled chest. "Dray... I think it might be better—"

"Jared, I know you think I don't know very much. But some things I do know about. I know about making love. I read about it all the time."

Jared was spellbound.

"And I want to try it—" Dray unzipped his pants. "—with you." He quickly removed his pants and underwear, showing the evidence that he was ready for the commitment. He walked to Jared, who was still holding his shirt in his hand—frozen. Dray took the shirt from him. "Do you want me to help you with your pants?" Innocence and desire combined.

Jared, lost in the depths of Dray's eyes, nodded, almost imperceptibly.

Dray unbuttoned Jared's jeans and slid them down his legs. Jared held rigid... everywhere. *I'm being seduced. By a virgin.* Then Dray slid his fingers into sides of Jared's briefs and caressed them down his legs.

Jared, full desire now on display, held his breath as Dray slowly rose to meet him face to face, their bodies now touching intimately, Dray's nose a mere inch from Jared's. Their Armagnac breaths commingled in a heady aroma.

"Jared? Will you teach me what to do? I know what I've read in books, but now that it's real, I feel kind of unsure. I want to do it right for you."

Jared nodded again, feeling that somehow *he* was about to learn a few things. And he sensed with every fiber of his being that it would be *right* with Dray.

Jared moved his lips slowly to Dray's. An actual spark popped between them and they flinched. *Static electricity?*

"Does that always happen?" Dray said in wonderment.

"Never."

"Oh," Dray responded, seeming to totally understand the phenomenon. He moved his lips to Jared's.

The spark was nothing compared to the electricity that was surging now through their bodies. Their arms naturally entwined around one another.

Jared drank in the most soul-scorching kiss of his life; their mouths opened simultaneously and their tongues met.

After several minutes, their lips parted. Dray said, "That was way better than what I read about. Is kissing always like this?

Once again, Jared responded with, "Never."

Dray nestled his head in the crook of Jared's neck, breathing in the scent of him. Jared held him, doing the same. "Jared?"

"Yes?"

"I know there's more, but could we lie down on the bed now, because if you let go of me I think I might fall down."

Jared laughed full-throatedly, and Dray joined in.

Jared fell straight back. Dray fell next to him and leaned on one elbow staring down at him. Their eyes locked and Dray reached out a tentative hand and placed it on Jared's chest. Jared sucked in a breath as the palm seared his flesh.

"I love your chest, Jared. It feels so warm and hard." Dray bent his head and licked a nipple. "It tastes good, too."

Jared decided at that very moment that this was to be his final act on earth. Dray was going to kill him with sex. If this first action of Dray's was any indication of what was to come, he was in for the ride of his life. If this was how he was going to go, he couldn't think of a better way. Dray bowed his head again and licked the other nipple, using his mouth to draw in the nub and suck. Jared involuntarily grabbed the back of Dray's head and pulled it to him, clutching for dear life. Dray kept up the action, while his wandering hands ran up and down Jared's sides, kneading and squeezing. Jared groaned and thought that he could not ever remember his nipples being so sensitive. *What would happen when Dray got lower on his body?*

He found out.

Dray had an innate sense for what would please Jared the most. His honest, uninhibited love-making could not be duplicated. His exploration, curiosity, and eagerness knew no bounds. And for the first time in Jared's life, neither did his. It made Jared question exactly what type of romances Dray had read.

Dray brought Jared close to climax several times but always seemed to know when to slow down, how to prolong the torturous ecstasy. Jared hoped the pleasure he was giving Dray in return could somewhere match the sensations he was feeling. He wanted it to be perfect for Dray. And he did seem to be enjoying it. Jared pulled out all the stops and let go.

As Jared peaked once again he heard Dray's voice in his ear, gasping, "This is perfect, Jared. You're perfect. I have to—"

Those simple honest words put Jared over the top as well. It was, well...

Perfect.

✳ ✳ ✳

Jared's peaceful dreaming was suddenly exploded by a scream from Dray, who lay in his arms.

"Noooo! Mom! Dad!" Dray was writhing and clutching at Jared. "Won't go! Save you!" A pause. "Fire! Noooo!" This last cry, the most heart wrenching of all.

Dray was silently crying on Jared's chest. Jared held him for dear life and slowly rubbed his back.

After several minutes, the crying stopped. "Jared?" A sniff.

"I'm here," Jared whispered, wanting to wipe his own tears away but afraid to break his hold. He would have sold his soul for

Dray to not have to endure this agony. Why did things like this have to happen to the innocent and good?

"I remember." A hushed statement.

Jared held his breath.

And then it came out. All of it. Like a reporter relaying the day's top stories, but in an eerily detached tone.

"My last name is Alcott. I live in Denver."

Alcott. The name was familiar.

"My father owns a private charter plane business. He flies a lot of important people places. We were going to our cabin in Vail, my mom and dad and I. I don't have any brothers or sisters. I heard my dad tell my mom one time that he didn't think it would be a good idea to have any more children because *it* might happen again. I didn't understand then, but I do now."

Jared stifled a sob. *Parents could be so cruel… and stupid.*

"The snowstorm came up fast. Dad said the forecast was clear, that it must be a freak storm. The engines started to make a funny noise. My dad said there must be too much snow in the propellers. He told my mom and me to strap in real tight. He was going to try to find a place to land. We couldn't make it to Vail. I could tell the plane was going down, and then I guess we hit a tree or something. All I could see was white. My mom screamed."

Jared could feel Dray's tears falling on his chest, but Dray went on, as if he couldn't help himself, as if his very life depended on relaying his tale.

"I hit my head on the window, I think, and then I don't

remember anything until I woke up on the ground in the snow. The plane was on fire and I could still see my mom sitting in her seat. The side of the plane was ripped away. I couldn't see my dad anywhere.

She yelled to me, "Run, Dray! Go! Go!" I tried to stand up and yelled to her, "No! No! I won't go!" I fell back down and the plane exploded. Everything went black again."

Jared felt Dray's arms tightening around him.

"When I woke up this time, the fire was out and what was left of the plane was almost covered with snow. I couldn't see my mom anymore."

Jared couldn't help it. His body jerked with a sob.

Dray squeezed Jared and didn't comment. "I walked and walked a long time, until I found you."

Jared sobbed again.

"It's okay, Jared." Dray squeezed him again.

Dray was comforting *him*?

"Things happen for reasons. We don't know why sometimes. They just do." He paused. "The crash led me to you."

Jared lost it. "Oh Dray..." Jared hugged him desperately, trying to squeeze away the pain. Both of theirs.

After a minute, Dray began again, unconsciously rubbing Jared's chest as he spoke. "I guess this is one of the bad parts of life my parents were trying to keep me from." He sniffled. "They took me out of school when I was six because the teacher said I was a slow learner and the kids were picking on me." He stopped. A memory. "They called me Dumb Dray. He pulled back to meet

Jared's eyes. "But I'm not dumb, Jared. I know that."

Jared's heart was ready to explode with grief for this poor, loving boy.

Dray continued, a touch of regret, not bitterness in his voice, "So they kept me home from school and away from other kids. I had a tutor, Evan. He was nice and I learned a lot, but I don't think my parents thought so. They told me what I could watch on TV, what to wear, what to read—not good books like yours—but boring books, like—"

"*The Red Badge of Courage,*" they said together. A bittersweet smile came to both their lips.

Jared's hand caressed Dray's face and brushed away some tears. "You don't have to tell me any more if you don't want to."

"I want to, Jared. I've never been able to tell anyone before. And I think you should know."

Jared was touched. Again.

"I hardly ever got to go anywhere, and if I did my parents always watched me closely or had someone else watch me." He stopped again. "I think I embarrassed them. I heard things they said to people on the phone or when we had guests at the house. They always thought I wasn't around, but I was. Now they're gone, Jared. I miss them. I know they weren't perfect, and they didn't understand me, but they loved me. They were always kind and gave me nice presents. They just needed to let me try some things on my own. Now I am alone, Jared. I don't have anyone..." And then he said very quietly, "But you." His breathing became agitated. "And now that you know everything about me, *you* probably don't want me either!" He tore away from Jared and began to sob uncontrollably into his pillow.

Jared overcome by this abrupt shift in Dray said, "That's not true." He tried to touch Dray's shoulder, but was violently thrown off. He tried to think of something to say to make Dray believe him as he listened to minute after minute of anguished crying, but nothing came to mind.

Finally, Dray's sobs ceased and he abruptly whirled to face Jared, his face harshly lit by the glow from the fireplace. "Why *would* you want me? I haven't got anything to give you. I've never been anywhere. I don't know *anything*. I'm just 'Dumb Dray!' You! *You* have everything. You're smart and handsome. You're a great big famous writer. You could have *anyone*. Why would you want me? I'm *nothing*." The fire in his eyes defied Jared to deny it.

Jared softly began, knowing now what he wanted say, "I don't have everything. I really have nothing. After Brad left me two years ago, I gave up. On writing, on life, on love. I didn't care anymore. About anything. I thought my life was over. My life was Brad, and I'd been betrayed. I didn't want to have anything to do with anyone ever again. I was pathetic. And then you appeared. An innocent, loving human being. You made me see that there can be beauty in others... in life... and in myself. You made me realize that my life shouldn't be dependent on someone else's. And truthfully, Brad and I hadn't been together as lovers for a long time. I just didn't want to see it or take part of the blame for it. A relationship is just that, a relationship, with both sides giving equally to the other.

"Brad and I were only giving to ourselves. I was just too naive or stupid to see it, but he did. I guess I should thank him for it. Otherwise I'd still be in an unloving relationship with both of us just growing farther and farther apart. Thanks, Brad." He smiled at Dray. "And now you've shown me something else. You've shown me that giving is better than receiving. That's what I never got. I always thought I should get something back. What an *idiot*. Thank you, Dray. And as for you being nothing... well, they're—*you're*—wrong! You're intelligent, sensitive, perceptive, honest... hot..."

"Hot?"

"Unbelievably."

The corners of Dray's mouth quirked up a little. "I think you're hot, too."

Jared pulled Dray into his arms. They just held each other for several minutes, punctuated by a sob or sniffle from both of them.

"Jared? What am I going to do?"

"Sleep. We can't do anything right now, until this snow lets up. Tomorrow we'll sort things out and take it from there."

"You're so smart, Jared. Good idea." Dray wriggled his body against Jared's.

"But it doesn't feel like you want to sleep."

"I may be smart, but you're a *genius*." Jared lowered his mouth to Dray's, determining that neither of them was tired just yet.

* * *

The next ten days saw more intermittent flurries and blizzard-like conditions. It seemed as if the snow would never stop. Dray was logically resigned to the fact that he couldn't do anything until he could get out of there. He had a few bouts of crying and moments of sadness, but overall he was bearing up with Jared's help. They worked out, watched movies, listened to music, and made love. Dray was always anxious, too, to read the latest installment of Jared's novel.

* * *

Jared had been writing fast and furiously and was now finished with the first draft. And thanks to the helpful criticisms and suggestions from Dray, he was very proud of the manuscript.

Dray sat on the chaise in the library, draped by Jared's arms, drinking Armagnac. He finished reading the last page of the manuscript and looked off into space.

"Well? Jared said anxiously.

"Why did you end it like that? I don't think Corey would do that, Jared."

Jared knew it, too! He had gone back and forth over the ending twenty times, and instead of going with his instinct, he'd copped out. *Dammit.*

Jared went to his desk and produced several pieces of paper. "Here's my original ending."

Dray sat and read.

"Perfect," Dray concluded. "Why did you write it that other way?"

"I wanted a happy ending." Jared shrugged. "How did you get to be so smart?"

"Sheltered life." Dray smiled. "Endings can't always be happy, Jared." He sobered now.

"Yes, they can. And here, this is for you." He handed Dray another piece of paper. "The dedication."

Dray's eyes filled with tears as he read. "Love?"

"Yes. I love you. I've loved you since I first saw your battered, bloodied, and beautiful face on my doorstep." He went to Dray, who embraced him fervently.

"I love you, too, Jared. But not like before. That was like friends. This... this... I feel this warm, fuzzy feeling... deep inside when I look at you or think about you... and it makes me happy."

"That sounds like a good description of love to me. Maybe I'll use it in my next book."

"It's not very creepy."

"Maybe I'll write a love story *with* a happy ending," Jared added.

"Can I help inspire you?" Dray said, snuggling intimately into Jared.

"You inspire me every day." Jared nudged back.

"Like now?"

Jared sucked in a breath. "Uh huh."

✳ ✳ ✳

Later in bed, cuddling in the afterglow, Dray broke the silence. "What would you do if I died?"

Mood gone, Jared's stomach clenched.

"Would you stop living again?" Dray continued, "Stop writing? Hate everyone in the world?"

"No," Jared said firmly And meant it. "I would continue to live, write, and most of all, love you. You taught me, taught me that I shouldn't have stopped living and loving before. And I love writing. I never should have stopped that."

"Yes, Jared. People die. But love never dies," Dray said with a somber tone.

Jared stared into the blue depths. "Your profoundness constantly surprises me." He considered his next question. "The snow has stopped. Do you want to go out tomorrow and see if we can find the plane?"

"You knew."

"You've been spending a lot of time looking out the window."

"It's pulling me, Jared. I need to see it. Is that bad?"

"No. Of course not. We'll go out tomorrow morning. I have lots of snow gear."

"Thank you." Dray snuggled into Jared. "I love you."

* * *

There was a note on the bed where Dray had been sleeping.

Dear Jared, I didn't want to wake you, but I had to go.

I'll be back. I promise. I love you.

Dray

Jared bolted from the bed, uselessly calling for Dray, knowing he wasn't there. Jared could always sense his presence. He furiously bundled himself in snow gear and went out in search of Dray.

Footprints led from the house out into the wild, but it had started to snow again.

Jared followed the prints for a mile or so and then the prints began to disappear as the snow filled them up. So he continued in the same direction, praying he was headed right.

* * *

After hours now of walking and backtracking, so *he* didn't get lost, Jared reluctantly went home. *He must be back by now. He promised.*

Night had settled in an hour before Jared staggered, semi-frozen, into the house. "Dray! Dray!" he called. Jared knew it was futile. He could sense Dray wasn't there.

Jared built a fire in *their* bedroom and sat by it, thawing, and staring into the flames. When the fire would get low, he would throw another log on and continue to stare and think as tears flowed heedlessly down his cheeks.

* * *

Jared awoke, shivering, in front of the extinguished fire. He was stiff and sore and… sad.

He walked the house aimlessly… Draylessly. Jared had reread the note a hundred times, "But I had to go." *Go where? Why?* Jared would go out and search again today, and every day, until he knew for sure… one way or the other.

He spent the next several days the same way. He would search during the day, and write at night. Writing kept his mind occupied, and he'd promised Dray he would continue writing. This next book might be his best one yet. Dray would love it.

If he would only come home to read it.

Then came the news.

Jared's road had finally been cleared and the local police had come to check up on him.

"Officer, has there been any report of a man being found around this area: thirty-three years old, good-looking, honey-colored hair, crystal-blue eyes," Jared blurted before the officer could even ask how he was.

"No. No one of that description has been reported. We were pretty lucky around here," the weathered officer said. "Folks bundled up and battened down when the snows got going."

"What about a plane crash?" Jared asked.

"Yep, there was one. Small plane. Musta got lost in the storm.

The Alcotts. Owned a charter service. Yep, a real tragedy. Coroner said they'd been dead a coupla weeks or more. Hard to tell when the bodies are burned and frozen. But we knew when the plane left, so we got a pretty good idea. Yep. Whole family gone."

"Family?" Jared's head snapped up.

"Yep. Father. Mother. Son. Folks only had the one child. Nice lookin' feller, accordin' to the picture in the paper. Yep. A real tragedy."

Dray. It couldn't be! "Do you recall the son's name?" Jared's whole body tightened.

"Funny kinda name... Gray... or Bray—"

"Dray." Jared said flatly.

"That's it." The officer nodded. "Know 'im? Sorry. Paper said he was kinda a special kid. You know, lived with his folks, didn't go out much. Special."

"Yeah... special." Jared looked off. "Thank you for coming by, Officer. I'm fine here." Jared closed the door.

"Anytime. Glad you're all right," said the muffled voice of the officer from behind the now closed door.

Jared drifted into the living room. Dray was dead. *Then who?* The questioned floated in the air. A ghost? The officer said he'd been dead for weeks. But it had only been a few days ago... He was going crazy, up here living alone. *Cabin fever. No. It was real. Dray was real.* Their love. Their lovemaking. He couldn't have imagined it. He could still smell Dray on the clothes he'd worn. On his sheets. *Everywhere.* How could he have written a novel and *dedicated* it to someone who was already *dead?* He knew Dray. Loved Dray. Would always love Dray. "Love never dies." Dray's prophetic words came back to haunt him now. "But you died, Dray!" Jared screamed. "You *died!* You promised you'd come back to me. You *promised."* Jared collapsed onto the sofa, curling into himself, and cried the bitter tears that only one who has lost his true love can cry.

* * *

"Don't cry, Jared."

Jared choked and gasped as a hand touched his shoulder.

"Please. Don't cry, Jared. I'm here."

"Dray?" Jared looked up into the most beautiful crystal-blue eyes he had ever seen. "How... what...?"

"I'm real, Jared. They sent me back."

"They?"

Dray looked up to the ceiling.

"Heaven?" Jared whispered.

"I think so." Dray sat next to Jared, still touching his shoulder. "It wasn't my time, Jared. I was thrown from the plane and I heard my mother tell me to run, and then there was the explosion... then I woke up and knew my parents were dead, but I didn't know that I was, too."

Jared was totally puzzled, and still thought he was hallucinating or dreaming or—

"They said I wasn't supposed to die. It was a mistake. That's why my spirit was still here. And it found you, as it was meant to. But I'd left my body. So, I had to find it. I told you in the note, sort of. And when I found my body, they took me."

"Where?" Jared was still in shock. "*They* made a mistake?"

"Up there somewhere. And yes, *they* make mistakes. Sometimes souls are very strong and they *know* that there is more they are meant for here on this Earth. Or someone they are meant for. So they sent me back. For you. For me. For both of us. And for what we still have to do in *this* existence. 'Love is the most powerful force in the universe.' They told me that. *They* like a happy ending, too. Love never dies, Jared. *I* told *you* that. It's true. Here I am. I love you, Jared."

Tears of joy streamed from Jared's eyes. He hugged Dray with all his might and love. "I want to hold you, and kiss you, and love you forever."

"You will."

They kissed a kiss for eternity.

LIBRA

Libra – The Scales

Traits: Diplomatic, Romantic, Charming, Easygoing, Peaceable, Sociable, Indecisive, Flirtatious, Self-indulgent, Easily Influenced

Argent Tanner stepped off the plane onto the tarmac at Kampala's poor excuse for an airport. He wiped his brow and could immediately feel the sweat start to run down his back.

Uganda!

What the fuck am I doing in Uganda? It's like going from the fucking frying pan into the fucking fire. Literally. I thought Afghanistan was bad. This is a fucking sweltering hell hole.

Argent, or Arge, as most people called him, had finally finished his military duty and was ready to start his life. Except now he was questioning his judgment. He'd closed his eyes and pointed to a country on a map of the African continent, and this was what he'd chosen. He'd heard of Uganda, of course, barely. He'd seen *The Last King of Scotland*, and knew about Idi Amin, but that was about it. Then when his buddy, who'd dropped him off at the airport, nonchalantly said, "Wow, Uganda. I hear they torture and kill the fags there," he knew he was in trouble.

Arge was just finally admitting to himself that he was gay. What he was going to do with that knowledge, he didn't know. Just like he didn't know what he was going to do with his life. "Fuck. I fucked up again," he said to no one as he went to claim his bags. *All right. Since I'm changing my life, I'm gonna change the way I talk. No more saying "fuck" all the time. I'm not in the Army anymore, and I'm not hanging around those guys whose every other word was "fuck." I'm not gonna do it.* He was happy with his resolution. *It's a start anyway.*

Arge took a cab—a dilapidated blue-and-white Isuzu with springs poking through everywhere in the back seat—to a small town a few miles away, paid the driver, and was left waiting at the pseudo-bus station for his next mode of transportation to the village he'd selected as his stopping point for his "Great Adventure." Being a medic, he thought perhaps he'd do some volunteer work while he figured out what he was going to do with his useless life.

The sun was brutal, and sweat soaked his armpits and muscular chest and back. His favorite (and only) pastime while he'd been on the Afghani camp was to spend several hours in the small, but serviceable, gym there. He'd managed to beef up his five-eleven frame from 160 to 180 pounds or so—all muscle. Now, he thought, the extra weight was probably making him hotter. He knew he would start losing some of his bulk, from sweat if nothing else. He wiped a hand on the back of his neck, removing some sweat, and felt the bristles from his recent Army haircut. His dirty-blond hair had gotten long, way beyond regulation, which he hadn't minded. Having some hair had been nice for a change. But he knew Africa would be hot, so he had opted for short hair—but not too short—short on the sides but with an inch or so on top in case he actually wanted to style it. Right now it was a little sweat-gelled spiky on top. *Not a bad look for me,* he'd noted in the men's room mirror at the airport.

He sat on a wooden bench, partially out of the sun, and waited. He should have taken off his khaki T-shirt (Army issue), but he didn't want to start his first day being sun-scorched. He gotten some color in Afghanistan, but it had mostly worn off, and he was afraid this African sun might just be a little harsher and not so forgiving on this *mzungu*, a Lugandan word the taxi-driver had used to describe any white-type person.

He waited and watched the locals bustling around the town—village would be more like it—as they went about their various jobs, some carrying baskets, some boxes, some bags, all in a hurried-like hustle to get God knew where.

"May I sit here?"

Arge looked up into the voice. The sun was in his eyes, but it didn't stop Arge's quick intake of breath. *It can't be. He's dead.* "What?" he managed to sputter out.

"I said, 'May I sit here?'" The man moved to the side, realizing Arge's eyes were being blinded by the sun.

Arge could see the man now. *It's not Clark, but it looks a helluva lot like him. Same muscular build, same sun-blonded short hair.* Arge judged him to be five-ten, five-eleven. The man proffered a hand.

"I'm Cole."

The same smile. That disarming, totally welcoming, smile. Arge found himself taking the man's hand. "Argent—Arge—everyone calls me that. Wow, another white guy. A *mzungu*. Right? What are you doing here? I'm trying to find—" He stopped. *What am I trying to find? I can't say myself.*

The man rescued him and his hand from Arge's grip, which Arge still pumped. "Nice to meet you. Argent. Latin for silver. Argentum, actually. I like languages. And I'm Greek. "Pila is my last name."

Cole? Clark? This is weird. "Nice to meet you," Arge said.

"Does that mean I can sit now?" Cole smiled.

"Oh fuck! Sorry. I mean... shit... I mean... sure, of course you can sit." Arge felt himself blush. "I didn't mean to swear. I'm trying to stop. Obviously I'm not doing a very good job of it. I just got—"

"Army. You're in the Army. Don't worry, you haven't offended my sensibilities. I know how raw the speech can get." He smiled once again. "And thank you for your service. Afghanistan?"

Arge nodded, taken in by Cole's almost beatific smile. "I just got out. For good. I was ARNG—Army Reserves National Guard— and my unit was deployed from Las Vegas. That's where I live—or lived—I don't know." He looked off into the distance.

"Las Vegas. That must be exciting. I've never been. I've been all over the world, but I seemed to have missed visiting there. I'd love to hear about it sometime, perhaps after we get to Ntenjeru."

"In-ten-what?" Arge said.

"In-ten-jer-oo. That's where you're going, right? I mean, that's where this bus goes, whenever it gets here." Another smile.

"Sure, that's where I'm going" It seemed like as good a place as any. At least now he would know someone there. And he found himself wanting to be with this man who bore such a striking resemblance to Clark. "You have a great smile," Arge found himself saying. "I'm sorry. I blurt out things sometimes."

"It's all right. Thank you." Cole smiled. "I probably do it too much."

"No. It's great. I like it. It's been a while since I've seen such a genuine one." Clark had smiled just like that. Arge could feel his eyes starting to mist.

Cole put a hand on Arge's forearm. "You've seen quite a bit of sadness." It was a statement, not a question.

"Yeah," Arge said, relieved that Cole assumed his tears were from his combat tour and didn't know their true source. He also found the warmth of the hand on his forearm comforting and had no desire to remove it. "It wasn't all bad. The guys in my unit were great. It was just time for me to move on with my life. And to get a life." He gave a little "hmph."

Cole squeezed Arge's forearm. "You'll find what you want. You're a good man."

A good man. You don't know me. "Thanks, I wish it were true."

"Don't be humble. No one could do what you have done and not be good. You will find your way." Cole squeezed once again and removed his hand.

Arge felt the removal almost as a loss. "Maybe you're right." For the first time in months, Arge had a glimmer of hope for himself. Maybe he would find "his way" and get out of the funk he'd been in. This man, this stranger, made him believe although he couldn't say why. "Who knows, maybe I'll be the next Faulkner."

"You're a writer?"

"Nah, I mean, I like to write, but I've never had anything published. I haven't even tried. I have ideas. Lots of ideas. But I don't know... it's not really a career. It's just... I don't know."

"I'm sure Poe and Fitzgerald and Hemingway all thought the same thing. I would love to read some of your things."

"I've never let anyone look at my stuff. It's probably not very good."

"Let me be the judge of that. Most great artists think their work is bad. I have a good eye for talent, if I do say so myself." Cole laughed. "Well, that was humble." He laughed again.

"Yeah, it was." Now Arge found himself joining in the laughter. When was the last time he'd laughed? Really laughed. He couldn't remember. Much too long. He'd always laughed and loved a good time. Then things changed. The laughter had gone from his life. *Clark.* His laughing stopped.

Cole touched his arm again. "It's all right. Things are going to get better for you now. I promise."

That comforting touch had done it again. Maybe this stranger, Cole, could help him. *A writer? Me? What do I have to lose? I thought I'd lost it all. I like this guy. He's smart, intuitive, and really good-looking. Square jaw, aquiline nose (Greek influence?), awesome smile, and exciting hazel eyes—half-mischievous, half-sensuous, that said, "I'm ready for adventure."* Well, so was he. He needed an adventure. He needed something. He put his hand over Cole's.

There was a tingle, a rush of excitement that portended more. But what? Their eyes met. Connecting. "Thank you," Arge said.

"You are welcome, my friend." Cole smiled. "Are you sure you're ready for this?"

Arge tried to decipher the intent of Cole's words. He stared at the man. "More than ready," he said, not caring the intent, only knowing he *needed* to do this.

"Me too," Cole said, removing his hand from Arge's arm. "The bus is here to take us on our new adventure."

Arge looked up at the approaching bus, which was even more dilapidated looking than the taxi he'd been in. How could he have missed hearing its approach? It had no muffler system and was stirring up a cloud of dust as it maneuvered down the narrow road, only partially keeping to the pavement.

The bus stopped before them and Arge found himself wanting to take Cole's hand as they climbed aboard. He didn't... but he wanted to. That was a start. He actually wanted something. For the first time in a long time, he wanted something.

No. Not something.

Someone.

During the bus ride, Arge discovered they were both working for the Village Health Team. Arge wasn't quite sure what all it entailed, but he knew he wanted to help people somehow, especially if he couldn't help himself.

"You'll see quite a bit here that is disturbing and disheartening," Cole said as the bus approached the village, which seemed to appear out of the jungle.

The dirt road for the last couple of miles had been jarring and made conversation difficult. The bus had no air conditioning, so the windows were kept open, but that let in all the road's dust. In the stifling heat, it was better to eat a little dust than pass out from heat exhaustion. Arge had eaten his fair share of dirt and dust in Afghanistan, so it really wasn't a new experience, although it had been one he would have preferred not to repeat. He coughed. "I'm prepared. From what I saw and read online, these people can use any kind of help we can give them."

"That is true, my friend. I think you can be of great help. You have a good heart and that is needed." Cole smiled. "I must also warn you that here in Uganda homosexuality is a crime punishable by death."

"It is?" Arge was shocked. "But I haven't... I've never... I don't..."

"Have I misinterpreted?" Cole said. "I'm sorry."

Determined, Arge said, "No, you haven't. But I've never acted on it. I'm trying to deal with it and find my way." Then he added, sotto voce, "I thought maybe you were..."

"Yes, I am," Cole said. "We're here."

Arge looked up at where "here" was: a two-story cement building with a few windows and a door. "Nice," was all he could muster.

Cole laughed. "It isn't much to look at on the outside. And not much to look at on the inside either."

"Wait," Arge said. "Are you staying here too?" Arge's mind started to ramble.

"Yes. The VHT only has this accommodation. I've been here a few weeks. There are only a few of us. As you know, the program is for four weeks and is limited. They've let me stay on longer. What made you decide to come here of all places?" Cole was maneuvering Arge's bags from the seat behind them where they'd been placed during the trip.

"Frankly, I looked online for some remote places to go to get away and figure things out, and I tossed a coin. Here I am, although if I'd done some—or any— research I probably wouldn't have chosen this place after what you told me about the politics." Arge grabbed his very full camouflage backpack and headed toward the front of the bus; Cole trailed with the other bag.

"I guess it was the Fates, then, deciding," Cole called from behind Arge.

"Yeah, the Fates."

They entered the concrete building. "We're up those steps on the left," Cole said, motioning and walking left through the starkly furnished room. "As you can see, the living conditions are minimal. The chairs are hard and the couches are lumpy... oh, and the table wobbles. But there are some good books on the shelves over there." He pointed to wall at the far end.

"I've lived in worse." Arge thought back to a previous posting, which had no couches or chairs, only dirt and ground for comfort. Any "pillows" were dug out sections of earth. This was plush.

At the top of the stairs, Cole said, "The rooms accommodate two. This first room is mine." He pointed to a door on the left. "The kitchen is next to me. There are two girls, Sharon and Jenelle, at the end of the hall, and another man, Burke, down two doors. They are out at the hospital at the moment. The shower is next to his room. Obviously, it is all coed. You may share with me, with Burke, or take one of the other two rooms at the end of the hall." Cole stepped into his room and set Arge's bag on the floor.

Arge walked in and saw the two small beds. A net canopy covered each. *Bugs. Malaria. Sleeping sickness. Welcome to Africa.* Arge smiled. *How do I say "I want to sleep with you" without saying "I want to sleep with you"?* "Uh, this is fine, if you don't mind. I'd like the company. And you're the only person I know."

"Good. I was hoping you'd say yes. I think it will be good for both of us. I don't snore and sleep pretty soundly. You'll get used to the night sounds here quickly. They can actually prove to be soothing and tranquilizing. I sleep there." Cole pointed to the far bed. "The books are my current reading material." He pointed to the small nightstand between the beds. "You can use the two lower dresser drawers and there is some room in the closet." He pointed to the open, recessed space on the wall next to Arge where a couple of shirts hung.

"This is all fine," Arge said. "I don't snore either, but... I sometimes have dreams... and I might talk a little bit." He closed his eyes and shook his head. "I'd better sleep down the hall."

"It's fine," Cole said, calmly. "Maybe I can help you battle your demons. I would like you to stay here with me."

The sincerity in Cole's voice convinced Arge. "Okay. Maybe you *can* help. We can try it. But if I get to be too much, let me know."

"Everything will be fine."

And Arge believed him... or at least wanted to believe him. He had some bad demons to deal with.

Arge unpacked and Cole helped him. When everything was put away, Arge ripped off his T-shirt and said, "I could probably use a shower. I guess you noticed that." He sniffed his T-shirt. "And this shirt and these pants need to be washed... or burned." He tossed the shirt on the floor and began to remove his pants.

Cole sat on his bed and watched as Arge disrobed. "Would you like me to leave and give you some privacy?" Cole's voice was very soft.

Arge had just pushed his briefs to the floor and stood up. Naked. He stared at Cole. The room suddenly became stifling and the temperature seemed to have gone up ten degrees. Arge could feel himself start to sweat as his eyes met Cole's. He subconsciously rubbed his hand over his now sweat-slicked chest. He felt he should cover his genitals, but that would have made it more awkward. "I'm sorry. I'm used to being naked in front of other guys. Barracks, you know, not much privacy. Does it bother you?"

Cole smiled. "Yes, but not in the way you mean. I am also comfortable with nudity. You have a very muscular body. And perhaps I shouldn't say this, but I am attracted to you. If that is a problem for you, you may sleep somewhere else."

Arge felt himself stir. He had not had sex in a very long time, other than with himself, and even that had been several days ago. And he'd never had sex with a man. His desire was strong. He definitely wanted to try it with this man Cole. But not now. He had too much to deal with. As his erection started, he knew he had to respond to Cole's statement. "I'm obviously attracted to you too." He half-laughed and stared down at himself, still awkwardly rubbing his chest. "But I don't think I'm ready yet. I have some things I need to work through. I'll go take my shower—a cold one—and then you can show me around. Okay?"

"Of course. We need to get to know one another. We will take our time. You are a good man, I can tell. And the showers *are* cold. I would show you the stall, but I would prefer not to stand just yet. Our predicaments our similar."

Arge felt a rush of heat, knowing that Cole sat there as hard as he was. His sudden urge was to rush over to Cole and rip his clothes off and see what was there. His eyes went inadvertently down Cole's body, to an obvious bulge. He thought that there was not water cold enough to get rid of the aching in his groin. "I'll find it." As he walked out the door, Cole called after him, "There is a towel in there for you. But it might not be quite large enough. I'll go have your clothes washed and return in a while."

Arge tried not groan, noting the reference Cole made to the size of his erection. "Thank you. I appreciate it."

Arge showered, soon not noticing the water's temperature. He'd showered in colder when it had been mid-winter in Afghanistan. Here in Uganda, the water was refreshing, in marked contrast to the humid heat. He showered longer than he needed to, contemplating his life and the future here with Cole. It seemed to be a foregone conclusion that they would hook up, as they had already both declared their mutual attraction. But Arge wasn't sure he wanted a hook-up. He wanted something substantial. Getting off he could do himself. He wanted to share something deeper. Cole was so like Clark in many ways. That was the big something he needed to deal with. But could he? He missed Clark so much. Even thinking now about what had happened made him tear up. It was so stupid and senseless. And his fault? He splashed water in his face to try to remove the hot tears. *Somehow I'll make it up to you, Clark. I swear it.*

"Here's some underwear for you," Cole said stepping into the small bathroom.

Arge had left the tattered shower curtain open for air circulation. Now Cole stopped and stared at him. "Feeling better?"

Arge wasn't sure if it was a reference to being clean or the fact that he didn't have a hard-on anymore. Arge needed not to think of the latter or he would find himself in the same situation again. "Yeah, it feels great to wash off the Ugandan dust and grime. The cold water actually feels good."

"I like it too."

Arge turned off the water.

"Here's your towel."

Arge sluiced water from his body and reached for the proffered towel. "Thanks."

"It seems you managed to keep in shape in Afghanistan," Cole said as he watched Arge dry himself.

"Yeah, believe it or not, they had small gym fixed up with some free weights. I got a little bigger than I wanted to. But I'm sure

I'll shrink back down for the month I'm here. There wasn't anything else to do on our off time, so I read and worked out. Wrote a little bit too. I'll put those on now." Arge referred to his briefs, which Cole had been holding for him while he dried.

"Here. Sorry, I was distracted." Cole handed Arge his briefs. Their hands touched. And stayed. The intimacy of that touch, combined with Arge's briefs in their hands, caused a sensuous connection between the men. Cole broke the moment. "You'd better put these on while they still fit."

Arge quickly donned them, realizing the veracity of the statement. He snapped the waistband and said, "All right, I'm ready for my tour of beautiful Ntenjeru."

"I assume you will be wearing more than that, although nudity here is quite common, especially with the children, so other than the color of your skin and your musculature, you would be pretty much unnoticed." Cole turned and left the bathroom.

"That's all I have are Tees and shorts, so that'll have to do." Then Arge added, "Did you clean my clothes already?"

"No, one of the ladies who helps us out is doing so. They will be ready later."

"Wow, laundry service. This isn't so bad after all."

"They will also do much cooking for us as well. If you are amenable to the local cuisine?"

"Believe me, I'm sure I've had worse. Our cooks on base would never have been contenders on *Top Chef.*

On the way to the clinic, where Arge would be helping, he

noticed actual mud and straw huts scattered among sections of the jungle. It seemed to be a mishmash of buildings. The occasional brick house and cement structures melded with the scenery. The trees were alive with birds, monkeys, and exotic butterflies, and the sounds were a cacophony of wonder. Arge felt like he'd stepped into a Tarzan movie. As they strolled along the red dirt road, he noticed the villagers noticing him. Some pointed and laughed, others just pointed.

"I knew you would cause a stir, Arge. It is a good thing you opted for more than underwear or the locals would want to come and touch you. They still may. And if they do, please don't be offended. Many of them are still fascinated with the white man here. They are all most welcoming, as they know we are here to help them," Cole said.

"I'm just as fascinated with them. I don't mind being touched." Arge threw a quick glance at Cole, wondering if he'd gotten the double meaning, for he wanted to be touched by Cole, and the anticipation of it was starting to occupy his thoughts more than he thought they should.

"I will remember that," Cole said and gave a brief pat on Arge's shoulder.

I guess he got my meaning. "Will the girls and Burke be at the clinic?" Arge asked.

"They should be. It's just up here on the left." Cole pointed to a white concrete building ahead of them. Several women waited outside the entrance with quite a few children around them. Most were under six, and most were naked.

"The mothers bring the children on Tuesdays to have them tested for AIDS. It is the number one problem here, and most of these children, unfortunately, will probably be positive. We will distribute the drugs as we may and be here to consult and console the mothers, a difficult task and often heartbreaking. But I'm sure you will be of great assistance, Arge."

"I hope so."

Arge found his heart breaking a little as he observed the mothers and their children throughout the day. He helped as much as he could, talking—or at least trying to talk—to the children. They were fascinated by his white skin and muscles. He would flex for them and make them laugh while they waited for their treatments. He met Sharon, Jenelle, and Burke and liked all three at once. The girls were pretty, Sharon was a little flirty with him, and Burke seemed like a good solid guy, with perhaps a little more-than-friendly interest in Jenelle. They worked together and seemed to have a great rapport. All three appeared to be in their early twenties. Sharon, with her short dark hair, he found out went to Harvard, and Burke, a dark curly-haired Irish type, and the very blond Jenelle were both from the West Coast: Burke at UC Berkley and Jenelle at UCLA. Arge was the "old man." They welcomed him warmly and assured him they could use his help.

"With those muscles, we know who to go to for the heavy lifting stuff," Sharon said and gave his biceps a squeeze.

"As a matter of fact, Army boy, there are a couple of crates out back that could use your muscles," Burke said, pointing to a door at the back of the building. "Bring them in here and put them on the table over there. And Cole told us you were Army. Afghanistan too. Thanks for your service. Now get the crates." He smiled and went back to the child waiting patiently for an exam.

Cole had left for a while, saying he had some errands and would return later. Arge jumped right in and found the time passing quickly. The line of patients never seemed to end. But, surprisingly, all the mothers and children were happy and smiling, as if they were on a field trip to the zoo. He couldn't help but admire their acceptance of the horrible situation. The people of Afghanistan—and for that matter the rest of the world—could take a few lessons from them. He found himself choking up more than once throughout the day as he looked into the beautiful, innocent dark faces.

"It doesn't get any easier," Sharon said at one point, noticing Arge wipe away a tear. "But we try to smile and keep up our spirits for them. That's all we can do."

"Yeah, I guess," Arge responded.

"We'll introduce you to the local mellower later tonight. It's rough, but it takes the edge off." Burke mimed toking a joint.

Arge hadn't smoked pot before, but if that's what they did... He wasn't in the Army anymore, so why not give it a shot? He'd ask Cole first if it was okay. And just then, Cole walked in.

"How are you holding up, my friend?" Cole clapped Arge on the shoulder and squeezed his trapezius muscle.

"Fine." Arge smiled at him. Everyone's been great and really helpful."

Sharon stepped in and squeezed Arge's biceps for perhaps the tenth time that afternoon. "Mr. Muscles is the one who's been helpful. He's like our personal slave. He does whatever we tell him to do."

"They are impressive," Cole said. "And I'm sure useful. *And* it's also time to call it a day. The line seems shorter and I'm sure you're all exhausted, as usual. You'll get used to it, Arge."

"I'm not sure about that. But I will do my best."

* * *

After dinner that night, Burke said, "How'd you like the local fare, Arge? I'm not sure there's enough protein for you to keep up your strength."

"It was fine and pretty tasty. I was telling Cole that I could probably lose a little muscle mass. I got bigger than I wanted to in Afghanistan. I'm too big."

"How could any man be too big?" Sharon quipped.

"Slut." Jenelle said and pushed her friend lightly on the shoulder.

"What?" Sharon feigned umbrage. "I like 'em big. Oh, *you* finally blushed." She pushed on Arge's chest. "I've been trying so hard all day. *Now* I know your sensitive spot." She laughed.

Arge felt himself grow redder and fumbled to change the subject. "I thought you were going to show me how the locals and you relax."

"Ah, the local 'vegetation,'" Burke said mysteriously and reached beneath his chair. He pulled out a brown paper bag then reached inside and removed a very large plastic bag filled with a green-brown, weedy substance. "Ta da!"

"Is this all right, Cole? Do you do it?" Arge turned to him.

"Occasionally. It's a bit harsh but plentiful and cheap." Cole winked at Arge. "You've never tried?"

"No." Arge hesitated. "My best friend always had a thing against it, so I didn't."

"Well, he's not here now..."

Arge bowed his head. Everyone was quiet, realizing something was wrong.

"Hey, you don't have to," Burke broke the silence.

"It's okay. I want to try it. Really." Arge half-smiled to reassure them he was all right.

"Okay, then. Let's light 'em up." Burke pulled out some papers and began to roll.

"Maybe this will loosen me up to start writing," Arge said, taking a joint from Burke. "Cole, ever since we talked about writing, I've had this urge to get back to it. Maybe it'll be cathartic. I always felt inspired when I drank. I guess the alcohol loosens up your brain as well as everything else."

"Maybe it will help." Cole watched as Arge took his first drag.

Arge coughed and choked a little. "Wow, this *is* rough."

"Yeah, well it's not the best grade. It burns some. But it does the trick," Burke said, taking a toke from the second joint he'd rolled. He inhaled. "Uganda's finest."

Arge took another drag, more carefully this time, and didn't choke. "I guess it's not too bad. Cole?"

"No thanks, I'll stick to my beer." Cole drank from the bottle he'd brought from the kitchen. "This works for me."

"Can I try it?" Arge held out his hand to Cole. "Is the beer any better than the pot?"

"I think so. It's Nile Special, a bit heavier and more potent than Bell Lager, the other local brew. Here try it." Cole handed the bottle to Arge.

"Mmm. I like it. A lot. Any more around?" Arge swallowed, imagining he could taste Cole's lips on the bottle. He guessed the pot had already gotten to him. His imagination was starting to flourish.

"I have one right here, just in case anyone else wanted one." Cole produced another beer from the floor next to him. "Anyone else?"

The group shook their heads. The girls were now off in a corner of the room, smoking and whispering.

The group hung out for another half hour until Cole suggested they all turn in. "And you have to be exhausted, Arge. It *is* your first day. Hopefully, you're mellowed enough to get a good night's sleep. Sometimes it takes a few days to get used to the night sounds and the heat."

"Sounds good." Arge stood up a little too fast and Cole grabbed him to support him.

"Whoa, big guy," Burke said. "All those muscles and a low tolerance."

"I'm usually good with beer. I am Army. It must be the weed." Arge still held fast to Cole. "I feel good, though. Just what I needed."

"Cole, you need help with muscle-man?" Burke said.

"No. He'll be fine." Cole began to guide Arge away from the group.

"Good. I might hang a bit longer with the girls and find out what they've been talking and giggling about." Burke got up and strolled away to the girls. "Good night, guys. Welcome to Uganda, Arge. Thanks for all the help."

"Sure. Thank *you* for everything today, Burke. You're a good guy. Good night," Arge said, letting Cole lead him away, enjoying the contact.

"Do you need help getting undressed?" Cole said, removing his own shirt as they'd entered the room.

Arge almost said yes, then stopped himself as he stared at Cole's bared torso.

Cole stopped undressing and watched as Arge moved to him, reaching out a hand.

Arge caressed the hard chest. "Great pecs." He looked into Cole's eyes. "They remind me of—"

Cole's lips covered his. Arge was lost in the sensation. His first male kiss. Cole's lips were soft as they moved over his own. Arge opened his mouth slightly and Cole accepted the invitation, slowly sliding his tongue into Arge's mouth.

Arge inhaled sharply and opened wider, letting his own tongue merge with Cole's.

Cole ran his hands under Arge's T-shirt and massaged the hard muscular back. Arge's own hands mimicked Cole's, exploring the defined musculature of Cole. His hands roamed sensuously as he enjoyed Cole's kneading of his own back. He slid his hands lower and clutched Cole's buttocks to him. Arge could feel the large arousal pressed against his own. He wanted more.

Cole slowly withdrew his lips from Arge's. "I think we both need some rest, Arge." He gently, but forcefully, pushed Arge's chest away from his.

Arge stepped back, a little unsteadily. "Yeah, I guess you're right. I shouldn't have kissed you."

"You didn't. I kissed you."

"Oh, yeah. You did." The corner of Arge's mouth quirked up. "Thanks. Good night." He slid off his shorts, revealing his still huge erection. "Ah, well, it'll go away." He looked down at himself, his body wavering unsteadily back and forth. "I think I'm wasted." He plopped onto the bed and fell back. "Shit." He flailed a hand in the air. "I didn't fix the netting. Can you do it for me, Cole? I don't think I can sit up." Arge felt like he'd been hit with a hammer. "And could you put my feet up on the bed too. Thanks."

Cole went over to him and lifted the heavy legs onto the bed, then secured the netting, to keep out the night invaders. "Good night, Arge."

"G'nite, Cole," Arge muttered, eyes now closed. "Great kiss."

"Yes. It was."

* * *

"NOOO! CLARK! NOOO!" The scream filled the night.

Cole dashed to Arge's bed, ripping aside the netting. He grabbed at the thrashing man, trying to get his arms around Arge's wide shoulders to stop the flailing. "Arge. Arge! It's all right. I'm here. I'm here. Shh. Shh. You're all right."

Arge stopped thrashing, almost eerily. "Clark? Clark? It's my fault. I'm sorry. I'm so sorry." Tears leaked from Arge's closed eyes. "So sorry," he wailed, chest heaving, breath coming in gasps.

"You're all right, Arge. It was a dream. Just a dream."

Arge's eyes slowly fluttered open. "Clark?"

"No, Arge, it's me, Cole."

"Cole? Oh, yeah. Cole." Arge leaned his head into Cole's chest and wrapped his arms around the man. Cole held him tight. Arge began to breathe deeply and was soon asleep.

Burke stood at the door, staring into the darkened room. "Is he okay?"

"Yes," Cole said. "War dreams, I guess."

"I told the girls I'd come make sure everything was all right. Is it? Cole? Are you two guys—"

"Let him sleep, Burke. Please."

"Be careful, Cole. Remember that guy they burned alive in the street in Kampala last week. That shit's real. Zero tolerance. I like you, Cole. Arge too. If you need my help, you know, a look-out or something, let me know. I won't say anything to the girls, even though I think Sharon kind of likes Arge."

"Thank you, Burke. We'll be all right."

"Okay, just remember, anything you need." Burke shut the door leaving the two men clutched together on the bed.

Cole held Arge for hours while he slept soundly, Cole eventually maneuvering himself onto the small bed so he could get some rest himself.

∗ ∗ ∗

The morning light found Arge naked and in Cole's arms, his head on Cole's chest, his arm draped over Cole's waist. He breathed in the scent of the man and snuggled closer, feeling safe for the first time... ever. He closed his eyes again, not wanting the moment to end.

"Everyone will be up soon. It would probably be a good idea if they didn't find us like this," Cole said to the top of Arge's head. "As nice as this is."

"Did I wake you? Did I have a nightmare? I'm sorry. I'll move to another room. I was hoping—"

"No. You'll stay right here. It's fine. It was nothing, really." Cole squeezed Arge to assure him.

"Thank you. I know it wasn't nothing or you wouldn't be cradling me in your arms like a baby. I don't know what to do. Did I say anything?"

"A couple of things. You said you were sorry and kept calling a name: Clark."

Arge stiffened.

"Do you want to tell me?" Cole said, stroking Arge's shoulder.

"I can't. Not now."

"Maybe you should write it down. Get it out of your system. Writing can be quite cathartic, I'm told."

"I don't know. Maybe. I need to do something. I'm so confused. What am I doing here? Uganda. Where they fucking kill people for what we're doing right now. I don't even *know* what I'm doing right now. I'm lying here with a man who's holding me and caressing me. This is all so fucking surreal. *Fuck!*" He pounded Cole on his chest. "I'm sorry. Did that hurt?"

"No, it wasn't that hard." Cole rubbed Arge's shoulder again. "Maybe that's why you're here, Arge. To figure things out."

"You know, I kind of think I am. I need to be lost. I need to be somewhere where I can just think and figure out myself. And what the fuck I'm doing with my life."

"You'll do it, Arge. I know. You're good man."

"Thank you, Cole. I need someone to tell me that. I mean, I know I was a good soldier and medic, but the rest I doubt."

"Don't. Remember, none of us is perfect. We do the best we can, follow our instincts, and trust that we've made the right choices."

"Well, the only choice I've made that feels right is this." Arge rubbed Cole's chest. "Lying here with you, holding you, talking to you—being honest for the first time. Feels right. Even if it is fucking Uganda. Shit. Sorry about the swearing. I swore I was going to try to curb my mouth. Army. I'll try to be better. I do have more of a vocabulary than you'd think. I was going to be an English major."

"Why'd you stop?"

"Army. I've thought about a lot of careers. Tried a few. Haven't stuck with any. I've taken a lot of college courses between deployments. Someday I may even get a degree. If I can ever figure out what the fuck I want to do. Sorry. I get frustrated with myself."

"You'll do it. I know."

"Thanks for the confidence. I guess we should get up. It'll take a few minutes for my 'situation' to resolve itself." He moved his hips indicating the firm arousal that had been pressed up against Cole's leg the entire time.

"Don't think I'm not in the same 'situation.'" Cole reached down to adjust himself in his boxers.

"I'm glad. Misery loves company." Arge nudged Cole out of the bed. "The cold shower should help a little. You can go first."

That afternoon they took a longboat on Lake Victoria to the isle of Damba. There were several small islands on the Lake they would visit to help with the VHT and to aid with HIV testing and awareness.

Arge made sure he wore plenty of sunscreen. Afghanistan had given him some color, but the brutal African sun, combined with the reflection off Lake Victoria, would scorch him. Even then, he still managed to get a little burn. They spent two days on the islands, and when they were finished, all of them were dog-tired, for in addition to travel to the various islands, they would also pick up coal or the occasional fisherman delivering his daily catch to the market. The Lake, of course, was the largest in Africa, and they spent two hours on it before returning to shore.

"Aren't you tired, Arge?" Cole said as they entered their room that evening and dumped their gear unceremoniously on Cole's bed. "You actually seem invigorated."

"No, I'm not tired. I've had two pretty good nights' sleep—no nightmares—helped deliver a baby, met some great people, and hopefully helped prevent more spread of disease. I feel like I might have made a difference."

"You definitely have. You and Burke and the girls are doing good work here. And you were great with the village children, especially when they circled you and kept shouting '*MZUNGU!* and tried to touch you. It was very gracious of you to take off your shirt and let them touch your muscles. They enjoyed it." Cole took off his T-shirt. "I did too."

Arge stripped off his shirt. "You mean like this?" The air in the room grew heavy. Arge gave his shirt a sniff. "Whew. Why didn't you tell me I smelled so much?"

"We all do." He sniffed his own shirt, mimicking Arge. "It comes with the territory." Cole dropped his shirt to the floor and took a step toward Arge. "And I don't mind it."

"Okay." The word spoke volumes as Arge too dropped his

T-shirt to the floor and opened his arms to Cole.

Cole took two more steps and countered Arge's embrace. They held each other silently and breathed in each other's musky scents.

Arge pulled his head back and locked eyes with Cole's. Arge opened his mouth. "I want you."

Cole's eyes darkened.

Arge pressed his lips to Cole's. And he was lost. Yet, at the same time, he felt he'd found something that had eluded him his whole life. The kiss deepened and Arge devoured Cole's mouth like a starving man. Cole responded in kind, iterating his own desperate need.

Arge mumbled, "What about the others?"

"We'll be fine. They always crash after these two-day visits. And Burke is watching out for us."

"He knows?"

"Yes. I think the girls do too. Didn't you notice how they've left us alone a lot the past couple of days?"

"Yeah, I did. Good. I thought things might get awkward with Sharon. I was getting the vibe from her."

"Who wouldn't give you the vibe? You're an incredibly attractive man, Arge."

"I think you're pretty hot too." Arge pulled Cole to him again for another kiss.

Now, there was no more talking, only moans and sighs of pleasure as they worked their hands and mouths over one another.

Shorts disappeared. Neither had worn underwear for the past few days; the heat and moisture was too much.

Arge pushed Cole back a couple of steps to view him, taking in the well-defined torso and arms. The slim hips and taut muscular legs. The defining manhood. Arge felt his desire and his own erection grow even more, wanting to devour the man all at once, and at the same time not knowing where to start.

Cole stared back, mirroring Arge's ravenous look, and sensing Arge's hesitation said, "Do whatever you want. I'm all yours."

That was the impetus Arge needed. He grabbed Cole by the shoulders and pushed him down onto the bed. He started at Cole's mouth, once again assaulting him with his lips and tongue. Then he moved down Cole's neck, leaving a light trail of saliva as he tasted the salty, slick flesh. He squeezed Cole's chest, licking and biting the taut nipples. Cole's arms were above his head allowing Arge free access to his adventurous tongue and mouth. Arge charged ahead, licking up and down one side then the other, creeping down ever closer to his goal.

Arge finally could not restrain himself any longer and had to know what it was like, what he had longed for. He opened his mouth and took in the man, welcoming the intrusion, savoring the sensation. Cole cried out. Arge indulged, spending lingering, excruciating minutes in exploration.

Arge felt hands on his head. "Not yet," was whispered. Arge stopped, then resumed moving down the rest of Cole's body, ending his exploration at Cole's toes, not missing an inch of flesh along the way.

He turned Cole over and began all over again. He lay atop him, bodies pressed close, but now something was different. Arge sensed an anticipation from Cole. Cole moved his hips into Arge's erection, and Arge knew then what he wanted. It was also what he wanted. He wanted to join with this man, to be with him fully. He lowered his full weight onto Cole, seared by the hot flesh pressed beneath his own, his full organ searching for succor.

"Please, Arge. I need you."

Arge slowly complied, savoring the sensation and relishing the magnificent man with him. He studied Cole's back and shoulders, watching the muscles flex, just like—

Clark. Just like Clark: the head, the shoulders, the back.

He stopped moving.

"What's wrong, Arge?" Cole whispered.

"This isn't right. I need to look at you, see your face. This is my first time. It has to be perfect. You're perfect, and I want everything else to be." He pulled back and allowed Cole to turn over and face him. "Yes, like this. You're so handsome and perfect." He slowly entered Cole, who repositioned himself to accommodate Arge. "Ahh. Yes, like this."

Arge leaned over and kissed Cole, his movements slow and rhythmic. Cole countered every nuance with his mouth and body.

Arge reached down between them and encompassed Cole, feeling him jerk abruptly. "Together," he mumbled into Cole's mouth. Cole nodded his head in understanding.

This was Cole. *This* was right. He'd made the right choice. There was no turning back. And he didn't want to. Ever. This man had changed him.

Arge felt the pressure building, and could feel it building in Cole as well as he worked harder with his hand and body. Their breaths quickened. Their kissing became more frantic and intense. They were both close to climax. They groaned and cried out in unison. Arge wanted it to be life-changing for both of them.

It was.

They lay silently in each other's arms, Cole's head on Arge's sweat-slicked chest. Arge felt he should say something, but didn't. He wanted to enjoy it all. He now understood afterglow. He knew he was glowing inside and out. It had been perfect. He was a novice at this. Not sex, but sex with a man. It was a totally different experience. A different kind of bonding. He felt more comfortable and more like himself. There were no expectations; he could just do what he wanted to and not have to perform. He'd always felt that way before with a woman, like he was outside himself, watching. Now he knew why. It hadn't been right. That was not the way he was made. This was right. Every instinct in him told him so. A sudden thought intruded: Then why hadn't it been right before with Clark? Why hadn't he made love with Clark? He was his best friend. Clark loved him, and he *did* love Clark too; he just couldn't commit... or tell him. Why couldn't he say it? Why couldn't he express his feelings? Clark was so disappointed that he could never say the words—to anyone. He'd wanted to and had almost told Clark he loved him many times.

And now it was too late. "Too late," he whispered aloud.

"What's too late, Arge?" Cole said, pulling his head up to look at him. "Why are you crying?"

Arge hadn't noticed the tears running down his cheeks. "I don't know."

"Arge, what's wrong? Did I do something?"

Arge heard the genuine concern in Cole's voice. He didn't want to hurt this man. But he needed to tell someone. He had to get it out. If he didn't tell Cole about Clark, he knew they could never go on—at least not honestly. Clark would always be between them, and Cole needed to know the awful thing he'd done.

"No, it's not you, Cole. You're perfect. It's me." He took a deep breath and pushed back a little from Cole. "I have to tell you something. It's about the dreams." He stopped.

"Arge, you can tell me anything. I *will* understand. I've been around a long time and have heard many stories." Cole looked deeply into Arge's eyes for several moments. He lay his head on Arge's chest before saying. "You can trust me."

Long time? Arge thought it an odd comment. But he knew instinctively he could trust him. He lay back on the pillow and squeezed Cole's shoulders for assurance. "I had a friend, my best friend, Clark. He lived in Las Vegas and was a singer, an entertainer. He was a great performer. He had an incredible voice and a personality to match. Everyone loved him because he loved everyone. He was always smiling and energetic. He was always ready and willing to do anything. He knew how to have fun anywhere with anybody. He'd never met a stranger. I'd never known anyone like him. He was a magnet and I was drawn to him, emotionally and physically, although I didn't want to admit it. He was handsome and well-built, blondish hair." Arge paused.

"Go ahead, Arge. You need this."

"He looked like you. Which makes all of this so hard for me. Now that I know you, I know you're different than he was. But there are many similarities as well. I do know that I want you, but with Clark I was never sure... if that makes any sense. I wasn't ready. He was though. He loved me. And never feared telling me so. We'd joke about being together—sexually I mean—but we never did anything. He would have done it in an instant, which is why I guess I didn't. I didn't know what would happen afterward. I was afraid to lose him if it didn't work out. I couldn't lose him. I needed him. He grounded me and kept me sane. I let the Army pressure me too. It was a joke that the guys all thought I was gay. Even though they knew I slept with girls, it didn't matter to them. Somehow, they knew what I was hiding. I'd laugh and joke back about it, and it didn't really bother me. There were a few guys in my unit I was attracted to, but I never pursued it. I was afraid.

"I was married—for a year—big mistake. She was young, so was I. I felt like I should try it. Then there was another girl. That lasted a couple of months, for me anyway. We'd have sex, but I was never really connected to it. Most of the time I'd think about sex with guys while I was doing it. Sometimes I'd think of Clark. I was so fucked up. I still am, but you're helping me. I now know more of who I am—and what I want—than ever before. Or at least in what direction to go. I like girls fine, but my emotions and physical attractions are more for men—which I'm fine with. But I still don't know what I want to do with my life. I have been writing, like you suggested—another thing Clark always encouraged me to do. He was kind of a zealot about it. He really thought I had greatness in me. But I kept putting it off. Then, of course, I got deployed. He even encouraged me to write while I was away. And now you seem to think I should be writing too so… I've been squeezing in time here and there. It's on my laptop, and I'd like you to look at it, if you still want to. I like what I've written and I really enjoy doing it."

"I would love to. Please go on."

"Okay. Clark knew my wife and also my girlfriend after her, and they both loved him. As I said, everyone did.

"Then I got deployed. My girlfriend left me, finally. Being deployed was the perfect excuse. Although, while I was gone, she e-mailed me about maybe getting back together and trying again after I got back, which I knew I didn't want. My ex-wife was incommunicado. And all I really had was Clark. He flipped out when I told him I was going. I knew he would. It was so hard hurting him. He was the last person I told. I knew he would take it the worst. I was right. Ranting. Crying. The whole nine yards. I'd been in Iraq before I'd met him… but that was just it. It was *before* I'd met him, so he could deal with that. Now, I was leaving *him,* he said, and he was destroyed, which made it hard for me. I didn't want to go, but what could I do? They called my unit up.

"Finally, after lots of tears and reassurances, he came to terms with my leaving. I had to promise to call when I could, especially birthdays and Christmas and Thanksgiving... and any other holiday he could think of, including Groundhog Day. I told him I would try my best, but that it was hard from the base to make calls. There was only one place to call from and it was hard to get the use of it. It was supposed to be used for emergencies. I told him we could e-mail, as I thought there might be internet available. He said he would e-mail every day. I told him I would try my best. And I meant it. I wanted, for the first time in my life, to keep that contact with somebody. I never felt the urge to do it with my family, but with Clark I did. He was something... special." Arge stopped as his voice broke.

"You don't have to go on, Arge. Maybe you could write it all down?"

"I have," Arge said, sniffing a little. "I wrote about my experiences in Afghanistan, almost like a journal. But I tried to keep it entertaining and not just a day-to-day description of things. It was kind of cathartic getting it all out, and it gave me something to do to occupy my down time. I would send it to Clark in e-mails and he would critique me. Mostly he loved it, and after I was finished with my tour, he said I should publish it. He was so encouraging, and I found I really enjoyed it, which made me change the way I would think when I was out every day patrolling. I would watch for things that I thought would be interesting reading. I just had to make sure I didn't lose my focus on my job. It could've had tragic consequences. I also wrote about Clark and how I felt about him, and us. That was stuff I never sent him. Now I wish I had. Which is why I think I can talk about him now. I got it out and faced it in print. As I was saying, Clark was special. I'd never met anyone who was so selfless or caring—and it wasn't because he loved me. He was like that to everyone. Sometimes it would even make me jealous, although I never told him that outright. I'd joke about his 'new boyfriend' or new 'best friend' or 'fuck buddy,' and he'd laugh, but I think he knew I was jealous. He was really smart. He knew, for whatever reason, we couldn't be together. I miss him so much." Arge stopped again.

Cole rubbed Arge's chest. "What happened to him?"

Arge took a deep breath. "I had a motorcycle that he wanted to ride on with me so badly. It was crazy, and for some idiotic reason I wouldn't let him. I told him only girls that put out could ride with me. It was stupid. I told him guys didn't ride with other guys, which was even *more* stupid. He called me out on it and said he saw two guys on bikes all the time—which of course is true. I guess I didn't let him because of the intimacy of it. I was afraid that if he was holding on to me, he would somehow know how I felt about him."

"How did you feel about him?" Cole asked, still lightly caressing Arge's body.

"I loved him," Arge's voice broke and he let out a sob. "I've never said that out loud. But it's true. I could never say it to him. I couldn't even tell him he was my best friend. How fucked up is that? He knew he was, but he wanted me to say it out loud. It meant so much to him. And 'I Love You.' Why couldn't I just say it? He said it to me many times, and I would always hear the expectation in his voice after he did, waiting for me to say those three little words. One time, when I called him for his birthday, I said, "Me too," after he'd said, "I love you." That's as close as I got. *Fuck!* Why couldn't I say it?"

"Arge, you didn't have to. Clark knew, as you said. Some people do like to hear it spoken. It gives them a reassurance and more of a connection. Most people I've met like to hear it. And if you do feel it—voice it. It's not some dark secret to keep to yourself. It is something to be shared. Love is meant to be shared. It's the strongest force in the universe. It has, and can, change events and history. Don't keep your feelings to yourself. Let those you love know it, before it's too late and you regret it. You and your life will be much richer for it. I have seen it change lives many times over the years. Believe me. Now, please continue."

"I let him keep my bike for me while I was gone. Then a few months into my deployment, he e-mailed me that he'd gotten his motorcycle license and that now we could ride together when I get back. He took his test, passed, and told me he could now take my bike out for periodic rides to keep it warmed up till I got back. I e-mailed him that I'd rather he didn't. My bike was pretty powerful and might be too much for him just starting out.

"He didn't e-mail me back.

"A few days later, I got an e-mail from a friend of mine. Clark had taken my bike out. Clark knew I loved my bike and he wanted to have that attachment to me. He knew I wouldn't let him ride with me, so he did the next best thing. There was some drunk who forced him off the road and down an embankment." Arge started to sob again. "*Why didn't I fucking let him ride with me?* I killed him. My best friend. I killed him!" Arge squeezed Cole hard, and he sobbed harder, deep racking cries that seemed to grow more and more intense, while he let out his months of agonizing sorrow, regret, and guilt.

Cole let him cry and held on to him.

An hour passed. Two.

Arge finally began to calm. Every emotion had drained from him.

Cole had been silent the entire time.

Arge wiped at his face. "Thank you."

"You're welcome."

"I didn't kill him."

"No."

"I should have told him I loved him."

"Yes."

"He wrote me a letter. Handwrote it. He gave it to me when I left. He said I couldn't read it until I was missing him. I didn't read it till after the accident, even though I was missing him long before that. I thought I'd lost it. I knew I'd stuffed it in my pack, but when I went to find it, it wasn't there. I looked everywhere for it. Clark never asked me about it, so I didn't have to tell him I'd lost it. Now I wished I had. He could have sent me another one or e-mailed it. But I did find it, the day after I found out about the accident. It was right where I'd thought I'd put it originally, in the side pouch of my pack. It was really weird. I'd like you to read it. I want you to know and to understand everything."

Arge reached over Clark into the side stand drawer and pulled out a book. In the pages was the letter. "Here. Read it out loud please, if you don't mind."

"All right." Cole opened the letter.

My Arge,

I miss you. You haven't even left yet and I miss you. I need you to know everything, in case (God forbid!), something happens—to either of us.

You know you are my best friend (I've said it enough times) and I know I'm yours. (Even though you refuse to say it. That I'll never get.) But I need to tell you something, something I've tried hard to tell you many times, but the timing was always wrong. Or maybe I was afraid I would lose you. Which I couldn't take. I know I'm not the one for you. You're not ready yet. But you will be one day, just not with me. Something is missing for you. Maybe we're too good of friends. I don't know if I'm going to be here when you get back. And please get back. I need you to promise me that. I want to know that you are going to go on and become a great writer or whatever it is you want to do. Writing's got my vote, though. I think you're terrific. And (sorry) I've shown your stuff to some other people, people that could really help you with your career. They've all said you are really good and could even be great. I've given them your contacts. One more promise to exact from you and then I'll stop. Promise me that you'll find someone who loves you the way I did. I know that sounds really conceited, but be honest, could anyone love you more than I do? No, I'll answer for you. I don't even care if it's a girl. (That's a lie.) But find someone who understands you and that you can be honest with and share things with. Don't settle or compromise. I know it'll be a guy. Only another guy could truly get you. You're definitely not easy. That's why the girls didn't work out. (Also because guys' bodies are hotter.) Bottom line: be true to yourself. Don't let your other friends or family or the fucking Army (Yeah, still bitter) influence you.

Trust yourself. Something you've never done. You've got great instincts. You just never trust them. You've learned so many things since I've known you. How could you not learn this? Haven't I shown you enough times? Don't fight it. Go with it. If there is one thing I have learned and want you to learn, it's this. When you meet that special person, you'll know it. I knew it. With you. It just wasn't meant to be. But I don't regret any of it. (Lie again. Maybe the sex part.) But I would not trade one day I've spent with you for anything. You made me truly happy. Now please don't disappoint me and disregard what I'm telling you. (Yes, this is guilt.) I will haunt you forever. (You know I believe in that stuff.) Final thing: When you find The One, tell him how much you love him. Say to him every day (For you don't know what tomorrow brings.) "I LOVE YOU." When it is right you will know it, and you will feel an unbelievable release of feeling and emotion. It worked for me. Sergeant Argent Tanner: I LOVE YOU.

Forever,

Clark

Arge had been crying silently the entire time. He looked up to the ceiling, picturing Clark, and said, "He knew he was going to die. I don't know how, but he did. That's why he gave me the letter, to help me and encourage me once again." He looked up to the ceiling. "Clark, you are my best friend and... I love you."

Cole put down the letter and held Arge quietly for several minutes.

"Do you feel better?" Cole asked.

"Yeah. I do. Surprisingly, I do. I wanted you to know about him." Arge wiped at his cheeks once again and pulled Cole up to him. Their eyes met. "You did this. You brought this out of me. Thank you."

"I only listened, Arge. You did it. And I think your friend Clark helped you too. He was a very insightful man. You are lucky to have found each other. We are led to certain people throughout our lives, and even though sometimes the encounter may be brief, we can learn so much from it. You've learned and grown."

Arge looked into Cole's eyes and made the only decision he could. He trusted his instincts. He pressed his lips to Cole's and they kissed, only this time the kiss was so much more. There was passion, but also something else—a bonding, an understanding.

Cole ended the kiss and said, "You have also helped me. I have been searching... searching for a long time. I have known many people and have helped and guided them, some perhaps you have heard of, but I have never found someone to help me—someone I felt the elusive, eternal connection to. Many of my brothers and sisters have found it, but I never have. And I thought I never would. Please do not ask me to explain. At the moment, I can't. In the future, we will discuss this and many other things. Right now we need to rest. I will always be here for you." Cole put his head back on Arge's chest and closed his eyes.

Arge hugged him close, then closer still, and felt an enormous weight and pressure release from him. Tears sprang to his eyes once again, not tears of grief but tears of joy. He was going to be all right. He whispered to the night, "Thank you, Clark." He kissed the top of Cole's head. "Thank you, Cole."

* * *

Three weeks flew by. Arge and Cole were always together. They worked together by day, slept together and explored each other by night, neither ever too tired to indulge in one another, always energized to be together, to make love and share their deepest emotions. They went to the clinic and the islands and anywhere they were needed. Burke and the girls were right there with them, a team, with Cole as their leader and mentor, tackling anything and everything that came their way. It was a rare combination, and it worked. They all came to truly love and trust one another. The villagers even felt their energy and drive and would help in any way they could.

They gave hope to the afflicted, and their positive energy became a contagion all on its own. The Ugandans, for the first time, felt that they weren't doomed. They began to spread the word to everyone that they could be saved, and that the "*mzungu*" were their saviors.

"This is just insane," Burke said as they all walked back from the clinic after one very exhausting night.

"I know," Sharon said. "It's like we're Christ healing the diseased."

"You're Jewish," Jenelle noted.

"I know! Maybe I need to rethink things here." Sharon wiped the sweat from her brow.

"It's you, Cole," Burke said. "You've done something to us all."

"I cannot take any credit. I am part of your team. I *will* say that it is a dream team. You all have made your own contributions."

"It's Arge," Sharon intruded. "Ever since he came, things have been different. It's not just the two of you hooking up either. We all love that you two guys have found true love. It's awesome. But it's more than that. Arge, you changed us all. Yeah, I was hot for you at first, and I'm still hot for you, but in a different way. You're an inspiration."

"Thank you, Sharon. And I truly care for you all, but Burke was right. It's Cole. He's the inspiration. He changed my life, and just to prove it, I'm going to say something I've never said before."

The grouped stopped walking and stared at Arge. Silence. The jungle sounds had ceased.

"Cole, I love you. And if you don't love me, I'll be okay. You have taught me so much. You've taught me how to love and share and care. You've opened up something in me I thought was dead. I'd turned off all my feelings. Now, I'm inspired. For the first time. I'm writing and loving it, and even if that doesn't work out, I know there's more. I'm going to make it." Arge grabbed Cole by the shoulders. "I just lied. I won't be okay if you don't love me. Now I know how Clark felt. I have to hear it. I need you to say you love me.

Oh my God, is this karma or what." Arge pulled Cole's face to his. "Please, Cole."

"Tell him," Burke said as he sniffled. The girls couldn't speak because they were both crying and incapable of speech.

"Arge, there are things I need to tell you. Not here and not now. I'm sorry." Cole pushed away from Arge.

"Fuck!" Burke said and stormed off down the road.

The girls wiped at their faces and followed him.

"I understand," Arge said through the enormous lump in his throat, not understanding. "Let's go."

They walked the rest of the way in silence, Arge not even glancing at him.

Dinner that evening was awkward. No one spoke of much, and after the last hurried swallow of food, everyone mumbled, "Good night."

Cole removed his last vestige of clothing, stood naked, and said to Arge's back, "Good night," and slipped into the bed that had not been used since the first night Arge and he made love.

Arge shucked his shorts, and also standing naked, turned and said, "This is our bed." He stood full-frontal to Cole. Open. Vulnerable.

Cole stared at him from his bed.

Arge slipped under the netting of his own bed and held his arms spread open wide for Cole to join him.

Cole obliged him, slipping under the net and joining him face to face.

Arge's arms encircled him. "Now tell me. What is it?"

"I—"

BLAM!!!! A gunshot.

Arge covered Cole with his body.

Sharon flew into the room. "Arge, come with me!"

Arge jumped off Cole and followed her out of the room as a naked Jenelle came flying in to the room and jumped into the bed with Cole.

He went into Sharon's room, where she stripped off her shorts and top. "In the bed," she ordered.

He obeyed, genitals flying. Sharon joined him and threw her arms around him. Then, moments later, the door flew open and two very dark Ugandan soldiers with rifles ready entered their room.

"*What the fuck?*" Sharon shrieked.

The soldiers stared and mumbled something in Lugandan and backed out of the room.

"Stay quiet," Sharon instructed.

They heard more yelling from the soldiers.

Burke's voice.

Jenelle's whine.

Silence.

Arge could hear his and Sharon's heavy breathing. "I think they're gone," she said.

"I have to see Cole," Arge said, throwing back covers and netting.

Arge flew into his room. Jenelle was just standing from Cole's and his bed, still naked.

"The things I do for friends," Jenelle said, trying to cover her breasts and bending down to grab someone's T-shirt from the floor. She grabbed a pair of discarded shorts as well and threw them at Arge. "Cover that big thing."

Arge caught the shorts and held them in front of him. "Are you all right?" he said to Cole. "Thank you, Jenelle."

"No problem. Just glad you're gay. We've been expecting some kind of law enforcement to come along. You two are pretty obvious, in case you didn't know." Jenelle pulled Arge's T-shirt over herself. "At least that covers something. Great nightshirt, big guy. I think I'll keep it."

Arge said, "It's all yours. That's what this was about? Someone said something about Cole and me?"

"Yep." Jenelle said. "Remember that gay guy that got burned alive in the streets a few weeks ago? They're not messing around here."

"Oh my God. Cole, Jenelle, I'm so sorry. It's all my fault." Arge sat next to Cole on the bed and put his head in his hands, shorts hanging over his crotch.

"Don't be stupid," Burke said poking his head in the doorway, a frantic Sharon by his side. "These people, this government is the problem. They're not even Third World in their thinking. It's more like Tenth World. But we're here and this is what we have to deal with. And we did. We're a team. Things are changing around the world. Some places are going to take a little longer. Next week, we're out of here. We can all go back and let people know what it's like here. Maybe we can help. If enough of us say something, we can make a difference. And that's enough of my political speech for one night. Come on, girls, let's leave the lovebirds alone. I think they need to talk." Burke turned to leave and the girls silently followed.

"Yes, we do," Arge said, turning to Cole.

Cole moved next to him on the bed, the sheet barely covering his genitals.

"And don't think your being naked and so tempting will distract me," Arge said, trying to keep a light yet serious tone. "There are too many unanswered questions."

"All right, Arge. This seems to be the time to talk. I will tell you honestly, for things have gone too far between us. I never thought that this could happen for me. I thought I was doomed for eternity."

"Okay, that's a little melodramatic."

"Not at all. I'm serious." Cole gave a look so tender to Arge that if he discovered that Cole was Jack the Ripper, he would have forgiven him. "I am a Muse."

"No doubt there," Arge said. "You've been an inspiration to me and all of us."

"I am Calliope. Muse of the arts. My name is an anagram. Cole Pila. I have had different names over the centuries."

"Centuries?" Arge stared, open-mouthed. "It can't be. And I thought all the muses were women."

"We are who we need to be. I come to those that are in need

and worthy."

"I'm worthy?" Arge asked, not really questioning Cole's origin but accepting it.

"More than. I was sent to you. You are destined for greatness."

"I doubt that. And who were these 'others' I might have heard of?"

Cole smiled. "Poe. Fitzgerald. Hemingway."

Arge's mouth dropped open. "Yeah, I've heard of them. You helped them? I'll never be in their league."

Cole smiled again.

Arge reeled at the thought. "But even if for some strange reason I am, what about... I mean the... making love part of it?"

"That's where it gets complicated. Once a Muse gets involved physically, it is hard to be objective about our goals. Our emotions begin to control our thoughts. It had already begun for me when I was in my other form, even though I wasn't physically involved."

Arge stared at the man, slowly comprehending.

Clark. "You're Clark."

"Yes. I was—am—Clark. All of what I told you was true in the letter. I knew you weren't ready for me yet, and I wanted so desperately to be with you that I tried again. I justified it by telling the higher-ups that you needed more time to nurture your writing gift and that a new presence in your life would be what you needed. They agreed and here I am again. I couldn't take my same form, but I chose something similar. I actually prefer this one." He smiled. "But once again I have made a mistake. Tonight never should have happened. The militia will now be watching us. It's good we are leaving soon, because sooner or later they would find us out. I endangered us all by letting my feelings for you show. I am truly sorry. That being said, my job is to inspire creativity, and you have been the perfect pupil. But, like Pygmalion and Galatea, I have fallen for my masterpiece."

"You love me?" Arge said, hesitantly.

"Do you doubt it? Yes, I love you, Arge. My time as a Muse is finished. There will be another muse to replace me, as has happened for millennia. But your love has given me what I have so long desired."

Arge could restrain himself no longer, and he pulled Cole into a soul-shattering kiss that he hoped would never end. "I love you. I love you. I love you," he kept repeating to Cole's mouth between kisses. "I'll love you for eternity."

"As will I, Arge, as will I."

A loud sob was heard from the hallway. The two men smiled at one another, silently acknowledging their friends listening from the hallway. Then they kissed to bind their future together.

ABOUT THE AUTHOR

Lance Taubold is the recipient of the IBPA Ben Franklin Award for BEST FIRST NON-FICTION for ON TWO FRONTS.. He has been an entertainer for 25 years, performing at the MET Opera, on Broadway and on television for 5 years on the soap opera "General Hospital." As a writer he has written for Envy Man magazine, both as a fiction writer and book reviewer. His first novel RIPPER A LOVE STORY was written with author Richard Devin.

Taubold is the author of the gay, paranormal romance series: ZODIAC LOVERS BOOKS 1-5.

Taubold has been a contributor to all of the award-winning NEVER FEAR horror anthologies, the UNCHARTED WORLDS-XENO ENCOUNTERS sci-fi anthology and has romance stories in ROMANTIC TIMES: VEGAS, and THE HAUNTED WEST. His next release is the gay romance, murder mystery MAGIC, MURDER AND MISTLETOE. He is currently writing a paranormal romance series with New York Times Bestselling author Heather Graham.

INVOKE BOOKS

Adventures in all Genres

Exciting Thrillers, Heart-Warming Romance,
Mind-Bending Horror, Sci-Fantasy
and
Educational Non-Fiction

InvokeBooks.com

facebook.com/InvokeBooksPublisher

Feed an Author...

Leave a Review

Never Fear Series

Indie Book Award Winner

New York Times bestselling authors, Heather Graham, F. Paul Wilson, Jon Land, Michael Stackpole, Matthew Costello, William F. Nolan and award-winning, master story tellers bring the best in tales of horror.

Never Fear
Shh… Something's Coming…

Never Fear – Phobias
Everyone Fears Something

Never Fear - Christmas Terrors
He Sees You When You're Sleeping…

Never Fear - The Tarot
Do You Really Want To Know…

Never Fear – Apocalypse
The End is Near…

RT Booklovers Presents: The Haunted West

Written especially for RT Booklovers, best-selling and award-winning authors Diana Gabaldon, Heather Graham, Virginia Henley, Kat Martin, Katherine Neville, Bobbi Smith, Tina Wainscott, Tina DeSalvo and more... take you on a time-traveling, spellbinding journey through America's sprawling West.

The Haunted West, Volume 1

The Haunted West, Volume 2

Romantic Times: Vegas

The Excelsior Hotel and Casino.in Las Vegas is the setting of these magical stories of romance. For decades the towering hotel has been the subject of incredible stories and rumors. Bestselling authors, Christina Skye, Heather Graham, Tina DeSalvo and a story by the Lady of Barrow, Kathryn Falk will take you deep into the heart of those, in the past, present and future... who roam the halls of the Excelsior in search of that perfect love.

Volume 1

Volume 2

Volume 3

Heather Graham's Christmas Treasures

Heather Graham's Haunted Treasures

Presented together for the first time, New York Times Bestselling Author, Heather Graham brings back three out-of-print Christmas classics that are sure to inspire, amaze, and warm your heart.

Heather Graham's Christmas Treasures also available in **Invoke Books Dyslexic Friendly**

New York Times Bestselling Author, Heather Graham brings back three tales of paranormal love and adventure.

The Third Hour

Winner of the USA Best Book Award - Thrillers

The Third Hour is an original spin on the religious-thriller genre, incorporating elements of science fiction along with the religious angle. Its strength lies in this originality, combined with an interesting take on real historical figures, who are made a part of the experiment at the heart of the novel.

Ripper – A Love Story

Prince Edward Albert Victor, The Duke of Clarence is Queen Victoria's favorite grandson and the most eligible bachelor in England. Coren Butler has captured his heart in the perfect Cinderella story. A dream come true. Then the nightmare begins.

Uncharted Worlds: Xeno Encounters

Uncharted Worlds—an exciting new speculative fiction series featuring bestselling and award-winning authors. Ten mind-boggling adventures include tales of ancient aliens, other worlds, and imagined futures.

On Two Fronts

IBPA Silver Medal Best Non-Fiction Award Winner

When two unlikely friends are separated by war, they must learn to cope with the effect it will have on their lives, their futures, and their relationship.

Bad Attitude/Diamond in the Rough

Bad Attitude Meet bad boy, undercover state trooper Reid Cameron. Meet Polly Sweet, the woman who is about to be his downfall. In order to catch a jewel thief, Cameron wants to use Polly's house, and he comes up with a plan, whereby they play at being lovers. But when the first play-acted kiss happens, neither one is ready for the feelings that kiss ignites or for the consequences that ensue.

Has this bad boy finally met his match? How Bad is Too Bad?

Diamond In The Rough-Detective Dan Murdock is on a dangerous stakeout, when advice columnist, Millie Gordon unwittingly shows up on the scene, putting them both in danger. To save her from possibly being shot when the mobsters arrive, Murdock jumps into Millie's car and throws himself over her to protect her, little realizing that the real danger starts when their bodies come together.

Romance and action are the name of the game in this two-in-one duo from bestselling author Doris Parmett.

Calendar Girl

Fate, it seems, has derailed destiny... and found a love for all time.
Tina Wainscott weaves a tale you'll not soon forget.

Family

Matthew Costello's widely acclaimed post-apocalyptic thriller, comes to it's amazing conclusion.

Treasures and Pleasures

A Collection of Romantic Novellas from the bestselling author Bobbi Smith.

Shadows in the Big Easy

Bouchercon Presents stories by up and coming Teen Writing Contest winners in this mystery anthology.

Stop Saying Yes – Negotiate!

Stop Saying Yes - Negotiate! is the perfect "on the go" guide for all negotiations. Fortune 500 Companies world-wide send out their teams of negotiators with copies tucked away in briefcases and notebooks... maybe you should too?

Do You Want To Be An Actor?

101 Answers To Your Questions About Breaking Into The Biz from people who know, Casting Directors, Producers, Directors and Agents tell it like it is.

Zodiac Lovers Series

In this series of romantic, gay, paranormal stories tales of love lost, love found, and love to last for eternity will fill your heart with awe and your eyes with tears.

Zodiac Lovers 1: Aquarius, Pisces, Aries

Zodiac Lovers 2: Taurus, Gemini, Cancer

Zodiac Lovers 3: Leo, Virgo, Libra

Zodiac Lovers 4: Scorpio, Sagittarius, Capricorn

Zodiac Lovers 5: Cetus, Ophiuchus